a one-legged cricket

For Mavis...
To new beginnings.
Discover yourself and
take flight

C. Macfenn
10/20/01

a one-legged cricket

c. j. macgenn

Writer's Showcase

San Jose New York Lincoln Shanghai

a one-legged cricket

Writer's Showcase
an imprint of iUniverse.com, Inc.

For information address:
iUniverse.com, Inc.
5220 S 16th, Ste. 200
Lincoln, NE 68512
www.iuniverse.com

Cover design by Robert S. Anderson, Matthew Wright, and Matthew Bail

ISBN: 0-595-16811-6

Printed in the United States of America

For my mother, Rose, with all my love,
and for Pops, who came along and loved us both.

"To everything there is a season…."

Ecclesiastes 3:1

Prologue

Julie Maxwell is sitting at her potter's wheel trying to center a wedge of clay. Tony is sitting very near her, watching her once nimble fingers now struggle with the clay. She grows more and more frustrated with each attempt. "I can't do this," she says, and crushes the mound of clay. She starts to get up from the wheel.

Tony stops her. "C'mon, Max." He reaches up and takes one of her finished pieces down from the shelf. He sets it on the table beside her and then runs his fingers over the form, touching it as if it he were touching her. "You love clay, Julie. You give it life."

"I can't do this, Tony. I can't pretend it matters anymore." Tony's weary eyes study Julie for a moment. "But it does matter. You have a gift, Jule."

She tries to get up from the wheel again, but Tony gently takes her hands and replaces them on the clay. "Promise me, Jule, promise me you won't let this slip away."

Julie shakes herself out of her reverie and rolls over on the sofa. She catches a sudden flash of movement out of the corner of her eye. It startles her, but only for a moment. She knows what is coming. And then it begins, that haunting, high trill that is the cricket's song. She is somehow comforted by it as she stares into the warm glow of the fire flickering in the woodstove. She just can't stop herself from remembering.

Before...

She seated herself at a pottery wheel, centered herself and took a deep breath. The wheel began to spin. As she began to work the clay, the sinewy strength in Julie Maxwell's long arms became evident. Her shoulders rounded, her back widened and she hovered over the wheel. The clay rose gracefully in her hands. Julie looked at her students, her hands never leaving the clay.

"See what happens? Your whole body's involved." An elegant and sensual form began taking shape on the wheel. "This is hard work, guys. You've got to feel what you're doing."

The rhythm and balance of Julie's body were in perfect harmony with the spinning wheel. Her students were mesmerized by the way the clay came alive in her hands, by how beautifully it responded to her touch.

"Your fingers have to be agile and sensitive and strong." She was so engrossed in what she was doing she didn't notice that her husband Tony was standing just outside the classroom door, watching her as though he were seeing her for the first time. Julie's students tightened the circle around her. All Tony could see then was the top of her head; all he could hear was the wheel and the wet clay spinning in her hands. And yet, he was as drawn into her spell as her students were.

As Julie finished up, her students were eager to try throwing something on their own. She made it look so easy. When the group broke up, and the students went to their own wheels, Julie was delighted to see Tony smiling in the doorway. He was holding up a set of keys. Julie's face ignited with excitement. With the flick of his head, he beckoned her to meet him outside. It was as if they were clandestine lovers about to catch a stolen moment. She gathered up her things and told her class, "You're on your own this afternoon. Leave it like you found it, help each other, and focus guys, focus."

*   *   *   *

Martin's Landing was a small northern California town. Really small. Once a very popular seacoast resort, it now drew only a modest summer vacation crowd. The houses and shops were old, quaint, and very weathered by the sea. The streets were paved, but more walkable than drivable, and the great Pacific Ocean was the backdrop for it all.

Tony and Julie's new home, 477 Oceanside Way, was a rustic cottage that overlooked a beautiful stretch of beach and rolling sand dunes. A giant matron of a tree hung over the little cottage like a protective mother. Tiny wild irises were in bloom everywhere. A "for sale" sign with a "sold" sticker slapped across it was posted near the walkway that led to the front door. Standing in the shadow of the majestic old eucalyptus tree, out behind the house, was a ramshackle little greenhouse.

Tony and Julie were eager to unload the car. Paint, drop cloths, brushes and a picnic basket—they had everything they needed. As they started toward the house, they heard the chirrup of a solitary cricket. They looked over at a large, leafy shrub. Another very vibrant chirrup emanated from within, and then the high melodic trill that was his song grew louder and louder. Tony and Julie drew nearer. The cricket sensed them and stopped. Then, with the suddenness of an exploding bullet, he sprang past them and disappeared into the grass. They laughed. Julie grabbed Tony, kissed him, and said, "I think it's good luck, crickets...or something like that."

As if they were newlyweds, Tony swept her off her feet, shoved the front door open and stepped through it. Inside, the house was U-shaped, with an old redwood deck neatly tucked in the center of it. It was all windows and sliding glass doors. Sunlight flooded the room and in every direction there was something wonderful to see—the ocean, the tree, the wild irises dotting the landscape like little purple and yellow paint splotches.

"Yes! This is our little piece of heaven," Julie said, as she slipped slowly out of his arms. They stood in silence for a moment, taking it all in.

Tony walked over to the window and looked out at the ocean. "And it's ours, all ours. We finally have our own home. God, this view, I can't wait to set my desk up. Who wouldn't be creative looking out at that?"

Julie wandered into the bedroom. She stood at the window and watched the tree swaying in the breeze. It seemed joyful to her, glad the wind was dancing with its leaves. "I want to wake up looking at that tree every morning for the rest of my life," she thought. She looked out at the little greenhouse. A sense of rapture came over her. She could hardly believe she was finally going to have her own studio.

Tony interrupted her interlude with the greenhouse and the tree when he marched into the room and rolled out his drop cloth. "We've got to get down to business here, Max, or we'll never get this place painted. And, since I'm the tallest, I'll do the rolling."

"Oh right, because you're the tallest."

"I thought you'd want to do the taping and trimming. Didn't you tell me that's where all the artistry is?"

"I did, but aren't we a two artist family now? I've got a great idea, let's flip for it."

Tony reached in his pocket and pulled out a coin, confidence written all over his face.

A sly grin crossed Julie's face. "Heads I do the walls, tails you do the trim."

Tony flipped the coin and while it was still in mid-air he realized he'd been duped. He tried to grab her in retaliation and they wrestled to the floor in a heap of arms, legs, and laughter.

"Okay, okay, I give," she squealed, "we can split it, even-steven." They cracked up again.

*   *   *   *

Later, while Julie was standing on a ladder finishing the trim along the top of the window, Tony was covertly watching her long, lean legs as she stretched to reach the top of the window. Something suddenly came over him. He bent over, filled his paint tray and dipped his paintbrush into the paint. He crept quietly over to the ladder and ever so delicately ran the tip of the brush up Julie's bare calf. It was a very sensual movement.

"Uhmmmm," she whispered, enjoying the feeling of the wet paintbrush moving up her leg.

"What do you think about that?" Tony asked.

After a moment, Julie smiled down at him, "I think you should do the other one."

Tony reached up and pulled her off the ladder, paint splashing everywhere. They kissed and tumbled to the floor in each other's arms. There, entwined on the floor, and covered with paint, Tony very deliberately dabbed the end of her nose with the paintbrush. "I love you Maxwell, and I'm going to pay you back for all these years."

"So pay me back now," she responded, and they kissed passionately.

Just as things were heating up, there was a knock at the door. They were tempted not to answer. They stalled for as long as they could, immersed in each other. But, the knocking only got louder and more persistent.

Ian and Annie MacFarland were just about to give up when finally, a bit breathless, and with paint everywhere, Tony and Julie answered the door. Ian and Annie stared at the two of them, and then looked at each other with mock surprise.

Ian was a warm, open, immediately likable kind of man—a commercial fisherman with that "salt of the sea" essence reminiscent of an Andrew Wyeth painting. Annie was a soft-spoken, slightly reserved, perfect complement to his outgoing nature. There was something pristine about her, like a clean, neatly pressed and sparkling white nurse's uniform.

Ian couldn't resist, "And what have you two been doing?"

"What do you think we were doing? We were painting," Julie demurred as she grabbed Annie's arm and pulled her into the kitchen.

"Each other maybe," Ian teased, as he and Tony headed off to tackle the greenhouse. Man's work.

*   *   *   *

In the kitchen, Julie and Annie were taping off the windows and getting ready to paint.

"Do you think you'll miss the university, Jule?"

"I don't know, I never really wanted to be a teacher, you know. I always meant to go out on my own. But then we met," Julie stopped what she was doing and looked out the window at her husband. She smiled for a second and then went on, "All I could think about was him. Then we got married and moved to the city and…."

"And there were bills to be paid and meals to be cooked," Annie chimed in.

They both rolled their eyes, like women do sometimes when they've been down the same road and they really understand each other.

Annie felt like pressing Julie a little, "Are you bitter about that? At all?"

That caught Julie off guard. She thought about it for a second. "Not really. It was much easier for me to put myself into the system and earn while my students learned than it was for Tony to work and try to write. Teaching was good for me, Annie. I'm a better potter because of it. I'm more confident now."

Annie smiled, "You've arrived, isn't that what they say?"

Julie laughed, "Yeah, that's what they say. But I feel more like I'm coming in for a landing!"

*   *   *   *

Ian was up on the greenhouse roof and Tony was trying to hoist some lumber up to him when suddenly Tony seemed to buckle under the weight of the wood. The lumber crashed onto him and slammed him to the ground.

"Getting pretty old there, buddy," Ian hollered down to him. Then he could see that his friend was unable to get up. Ian jumped down and tried to give Tony a hand. Tony was ashen gray and sweating profusely. Ian didn't understand what had happened.

"Tony, what's wrong? Did the 2 x 4 hit you?"

Tony tried to conceal his distress and struggled to get up. "No, no, it's all right. I'll be fine in a minute."

"You don't look fine. I'll get you some water man, just relax for a sec."

Tony didn't want to draw Julie's attention to his discomfort. "It's okay, I'm fine really. It just knocked the wind out of my sails."

Ian reluctantly climbed back up on the roof. He noticed how slowly Tony moved. It was so unlike him. Ian took up the slack, with one eye on what he was doing and the other on his friend's lack of vigor.

*   *   *   *

When Tony and Ian finished their work, the greenhouse had been transformed into an enchanting little workshop. An old-fashioned paned window framed the great tree, and the view beyond of the sea. Shelves lined the walls and a collection of Julie's work decorated them. Her porcelain forms were glasslike and the luminescence of her glazes seemed to light up the whole studio.

That evening, in celebration, the four friends gathered around Julie's new kiln, each with a brick in hand. Annie and Ian raised their bricks in a mock toast, "To our new neighbors." They then carefully put their bricks in place in the kiln.

Tony raised his brick and put it in its place. He turned to Julie and made a large, sweeping cavalier gesture, "For our new resident artist."

Everyone chimed in, "Here, here! Here, here!"

Julie had the look of a woman whose dream had just come true. She raised her brick as if it was the finest glass of champagne and then put it in the last remaining space. The kiln was done. Julie took Tony in her arms and kissed him deeply. "I love you Tony Maxwell, more than you'll ever know."

*   *   *   *

Julie was hard at work digging a hole in the dirt floor of her studio. It was a deep hole and she was covered with wet, sandy dirt. She was lost in concentration.

"Hey, what are you doing, digging to China?" Tony's voice startled her.

Julie jumped with fright even though she realized it was him. When she looked up and saw him still in his pajamas, hair all tousled and messy, sleep still heavy in his eyes, she smiled.

"Why not? It would be fitting."

"No really, Jule, what are you doing? It's five o'clock in the morning."

"I wanted to get this done before we put the flooring down," she said and went back to her digging. "There is an old oriental tradition among potters," she explained as she dug. "The father prepares the clay and then buries it a hole where it will age until his son is ready to use it. The longer the clay ages, the more refined and wonderful it is to work with. It is a way that potters can sort of stand on the shoulders of those that have gone before them."

"But you're not a father, or a son," Tony half teased her.

"I know silly, I'm doing it for good luck." She stopped digging and touched her heart. "I'm honoring the potter inside."

Tony smiled and then looked over and saw the enormous rectangle of fresh clay sitting on Julie's wedging table.

"When did you make that? In the middle of the night?"

Julie nodded. "While you were fast asleep. I did it in the moonlight."

She got up and went over to the clay. She ran her hands over it. "Feel it Tone, it's like a fine piece of silk. I love clay. Is that how you feel about words?"

"In a way, but with words it's what I hear. It's like they have music in them."

Julie wrapped the clay tightly in a black plastic tarp. When she was finished, she invited Tony to join her. "Help me with it, Tone. Let's bury it together."

As they were lifting the clay off of the table, a searing pain went through Tony's body. He gasped and went down on one knee, nearly dropping the clay. It was all he could do not to scream out. The blood drained from his face and he broke into a sweat. It frightened Julie.

"My God, Tony, what's wrong?" she asked him.

"It's nothing babe, really, just a charley horse. Let me breathe through it for a second. How much does this thing weigh?"

Julie didn't know what to do. She wanted to drop the clay and comfort her husband. After a moment, Tony regained his strength.

"You've been working too hard, Tony. You need to give the book a rest."

Tony grabbed her and tickled her ribs. "And I'm going to, because now you're gonna support me!"

They kissed and then buried the clay together.

*   *   *   *

The hospital was huge—one of those inner-city monoliths with long hallways, lots of fluorescent lighting, and shiny, shiny linoleum floors. Tony and Julie didn't speak. They hurried to make their appointment on time. When they got to the radiology department the nurse quickly escorted Tony away. She turned and told Julie, "You'll be able to watch if you want, once we are all set up."

Julie nodded, grateful for the nurse's kindness in this cold and unwelcoming place. A few moments later the nurse came back and led Julie down the hall to a glass window. The sight of the MRI tube made Julie's knees buckle a little. As the technicians rolled Tony into the tube, he looked over and winked at Julie. She loved that wink. It always made her feel like everything was going to be all right.

It seemed like it took a very long time to do the MRI. Julie stood at her post the entire time. When it was over and Tony came back into view, he was visibly shaken. He looked over to see if Julie was still there. This time he was looking for reassurance, not giving it. She touched her fingers to her lips and then to the glass that separated them. The nurses wheeled Tony out of sight and Julie went back to the waiting room. She didn't want to think about the look on Tony's face, it was very disturbing to her.

*   *   *   *

Dr. Jim Jamison started to speak and then stopped. He cleared his throat in an attempt to collect himself and then started again. "I'm afraid there is no easy way to tell you this. You have pancreatic cancer." Dr. Jamison looked down at his desk, "It's very serious, Tony. We have some therapies available now that might buy you some time, but…." Dr. Jamison's voice just seemed to fade into a deafening silence that filled the room. Tony and Julie could not look at each other.

*   *   *   *

The drive home from the doctor's office was a quiet one. Tony was driving; Julie sat staring out the window. Soft, sweet music played on the radio. The tears welled up in her eyes. As they spilled onto her cheeks, she turned and faced Tony. He raised his arm and beckoned for her to come closer. She collapsed against him and sobbed.

*   *   *   *

That night, as Tony and Julie were getting ready for bed, he opened the bedroom window. The field around the house was alive with the sound of crickets. As he climbed into bed, and reached up to turn out the bed lamp, he paused, listening to the night. "I think it was Nathaniel Hawthorne who said, 'If moonlight could be heard, it would sound like that.'"

Julie snuggled up against him, and clung to him like a frightened child.

*   *   *   *

Julie stood in the doorway of the studio, unwilling to go in. Tony gave her a little nudge from behind.

"Come on, Jule, you know you have to."

The studio didn't look the same now; the shelves were dusty and unkempt. The table was littered with unfinished forms. They were misshapen and heavy.

"I don't want to."

Tony leaned in close and put his face next to hers. "Come on, Max," he whispered in her ear, "we're trying to build a bridge here."

Julie reluctantly went to her wheel and tried to center a wedge of clay. The clay felt cold in her hands, really cold, and dead. She didn't like it. She grew more and more frustrated with each failed attempt. Finally, she crushed the mound of clay and tried to get up from the wheel.

Tony gently but firmly placed his hand on her arm and stopped her. "C'mon Max."

Tony reached up and took one of her finished pieces down from the shelf.

He set it on the table beside her and then ran his fingers over the form, touching it as if it he was touching her. "You love clay, Julie. You give it life."

"I can't do this, Tony. I can't pretend it matters anymore."

Tony's weary eyes studied Julie for a moment. "But it does matter. You have a gift, Jule."

She tried to get up from the wheel again, but Tony gently took her hands and placed them on the clay. "Promise me, Jule, promise me you won't let this slip away."

*   *   *   *

The beach was quiet and summer was ending. The season's colors were changing and the tourists had gone home. Julie stood in the sand dunes and watched Tony as he lumbered along the shore with a huge blue and yellow and green cellophane butterfly kite rising above him.

Tony stopped and turned around. He waved up at her and blew her a kiss. She could tell he was out of breath. He beckoned for her to follow him, then gathered up his strength and tried to race off down the beach. He was showing off just a little, and she was falling for it. He looked like a child, she felt like one. Julie hesitated, taking it all in. And then, she rushed headlong down the dune and onto the beach. When she caught up with him, he handed her the kite string. They ran together, laughing and watching the kite rise high into the sky above them.

Julie was so lost in the moment she didn't realize that Tony had stopped running beside her until he cried out, "Let it go, Max, let it go!"

She almost let the kite string go and then changed her mind. She looked up at the kite, glistening in the sunlight and fluttering along on the breeze, and then at her husband. She started to cry. "I can't, Tony, I can't let it go."

*   *   *   *

The winds of winter blew in from across the sea. Storm clouds tumbled in from the horizon like a giant quilt blanketing the sky. A candle burned in the bedroom window of 477 Oceanside Way. There was a singular cricket singing outside. Slowly the cricket's song faded and it began to rain.

Tony and Julie were alone in the house. That was the way Tony wanted it. Even though she was afraid, it was more right than Julie ever imagined it could be. She sat beside the bed, her arm outstretched, clinging to the warmth of his hand in hers. As she looked at him through her silent tears, images of their life together flashed in her mind like snapshots. She moved into the life of her memories and relived their love—the homecoming game the year they met—wearing the colors of opposing teams, but cheering together in the bleachers on the side of Tony's team; the two of them hovering over the scale at the post office, weighing Tony's first manuscript; their tenth anniversary; the miscarriage, no babies for them, and all the grief that brought; ice cream cones and bargain matinees—the warmth of her husband's hand, sharing things that moved him with his fingertips.

Sunrise, and the stark light of day, brought Julie back to the cold, now stiff hand that she was holding. She kept her eyes closed for a moment, letting the emptiness in the room settle around her. She could see Tony flying the butterfly kite down the beach away from her and watching, watching as it flew high, high, high into the sky. After a long while, she opened her eyes and looked at the body that was her husband. She stood, bent over him, and kissed him goodbye. As she walked out of the room, she heard the echo of his voice. "Promise me, Max, you won't let anything hold you back. Dare to be what you always wanted to be."

As she passed through the bedroom doorway, she moved from one world into another.

*   *   *   *

After...

Hours ran into days, days ran into weeks, and weeks ran into months. She didn't even know how long it had been anymore, just that it had been a long time and the pain was still there. She heard a long, low scream in her mind that never went away. It just echoed and echoed and echoed in her head. There wasn't any changing it. There wasn't any going back. It was so irreversible. That was the pain of it. There was no changing it, no going back and changing it.

Stretching out on the sofa and staring out the open glass door at the mammoth tree had become Julie's favorite pastime. She loved the tree. For months now it had been her only companion. She had come to know it well—its meandering branches, its changing hues, its many moods. Julie closed her eyes and listened. Birds were singing, the leaves were rustling, and in the distance was the rolling thunder of waves breaking against the shore. She settled into the symphony of sound that surrounded her. It seemed like the whole orchestration was happy sounding. Contrary, Julie thought, to her own unrelenting sadness.

"But you're not always happy," she thought to the tree. Julie remembered winter when the wind howled and the great matron was forced to bend and sway, when her branches were bowed and burdened by the storms, and her cracking and creaking sounds were so woeful and sad. "Too bad I'm a potter and not a poet,"

Julie thought, "I'd write about you, old tree. How you change and adapt, grow and accept." Potting made Julie think about work, and work made her think about how sick of working she was.

*   *   *   *

In her classroom at the university, Julie was lecturing before a group of students, one of whom was seated at a wheel. Julie was somber now, and distanced herself from her students with a professional veneer. "You don't push it and you don't pull it. You direct it, you just give it direction and guidance."

There was an obvious tension between the student at the wheel and Julie. The young girl looked up at Julie. "I know that is what I am supposed to be doing, Mrs. Maxwell, but obviously I am not getting it. Maybe if you could show me what you're talking about."

Julie started toward the wheel and then stopped. "I don't need to show you, practice is what you need. The only way you can master the wheel is to trust it and yourself—and by sitting there and doing it, over and over."

The student grew more and more irritated. "But if I saw you execute the technique just once, maybe I would be able to practice it."

Julie turned and walked back to her desk. "Tomorrow we'll work on formulating glazes, if any of you have pots that are ready...."

Under her breath, but audible enough for Julie to hear, the student mumbled, "Some great art teacher. How can anyone teach art from an ivory tower?"

Julie was stunned by what she heard. She couldn't speak so she signaled the end of class with the wave of her hand. As the students clamored past her, she stared at the student's wheel and the clay mound she left behind. When the classroom was empty, Julie moved toward the wheel. She stood over it for a long time, unable to reach out and touch the clay.

*   *   *   *

The pink slip in her teacher's mailbox, summoning her to the dean's office, alarmed Julie. She knew something was wrong and entered his office nervously. Dean Walter Clark was a large man, imposing in size but with a gentle demeanor. His tone was kind and almost apologetic. "Julie, you seem to be having a very hard time. I thought things would have leveled out for you by now. Maybe you came back to work too soon."

"I know. It's hard to explain Walter, but it seems like it gets worse as time goes by."

"Julie, you can't go on like you have been. We have to think of the students. Half the time they don't know whether you're going to be here or not, and when you are, well, you're just not at your best." He paused, trying to prepare Julie, and himself, with a moment of silence. Finally he sighed and said, "I'm sorry, Julie, but I've arranged for someone to take your place."

Julie was shocked by such a drastic a decision. "But Walt, I need this job. I don't know what I'll do if...."

Walter stood to dismiss her. He was almost as uncomfortable with the pain as Julie was. "Just consider this an extended leave of absence, Julie. Why don't you think about moving back into town, you'd be closer to your family. You might even want to consider getting a little professional help."

*   *   *   *

Annie was knocking on Julie's front door for a long time before Julie finally answered. Annie was disturbed by what she saw. Julie was disheveled, and in a state of despair. She tried to correct her appearance, half-heartedly running her hand through her hair. The two friends stared at each other. The atmosphere was so strained. Annie broke the silence first.

"Your mother called, you haven't been answering your phone. She's worried about you, Jule."

Julie didn't respond. She couldn't. She felt like she had stepped into a long dark hallway and she was too far in to turn back and not far enough in to come out the other side.

Annie went on, "It seems that Tony's agent has been trying to reach you. He sent you some papers a couple of months ago."

The look on Julie's face told Annie the papers were very important. She could see her friend struggling to focus her mind. Leaving the door ajar, and Annie just standing there, Julie turned and walked toward Tony's desk. It was a massive pile of papers, unopened letters, and unpaid bills.

As she stood over the mess, she started to cry. Annie was shocked by the chaos she saw before her, but she put her arms around Julie and tried to comfort her. Julie collapsed into the embrace.

"Julie, look, I'm pretty good with organizing things. You know, maybe we could tackle this together."

"I depended on him for everything, Annie. I don't know what I'm going to do. I don't even know where to begin." She slumped into his desk chair and tried to collect herself. She started rifling through the mess. As she dug deeper and deeper into the pile of papers, she became more and more lost in the maze that had become her life. Annie pulled up a chair, sat down beside her friend, and started helping her sort through the mess.

*　　　　*　　　　*　　　　*

Julie was seated at Tony's desk looking at all of the little stacks of paper that were neatly grouped together. It was so much more orderly now. She had to admit it made her feel less frantic. It was strange though. Tony had a particular way he liked to keep his desk, and this was not it. She was searching for a neat little place in her mind to put this whole desk thing when the phone rang. It was her mother. Without much ado, Mom liked to get right to the issues at hand. Julie listened for a moment, and then...

"I know you can't miss house payments, Momma.... I don't know what I'm going to do.... Yes, I made an appointment to see the bank manager tomorrow. He was very glad I finally got a hold of him.... I don't know where the money is. I'll find out when I talk to David.... No, I don't want you and Dad to come. I'll stop by and have lunch with you after.... Mom, please don't start in on me about moving again.... Ma, please.... I can't leave the beach. It would be like losing him all over again. Ma.... I'll see you tomorrow, okay? I love you too." Julie couldn't hang the phone up fast enough. She couldn't get up from the desk fast enough either.

She stared out the window at the old tree. "You're a survivor," she said to the tree. She looked out at the ocean. "Oh Tony, what am I going to do?"

*   *   *   *

The car window was open, the breeze was blowing through her hair, and she was trying to remember the last time she had driven all the way into the city. It might have been months. Suddenly, Julie caught sight of a flash of movement whizzing right past her line of vision, inside the car. It startled her. She squirmed around trying to avoid whatever it was that had just flown in the window. "Probably some creepy, crawling thing with a huge stinger," she thought to herself. She glanced quickly around the car, trying to spot it, but to no avail.

Just beyond of her line of vision, on the floor beneath her, was a bug. It was a cricket. He was stunned. Everything seemed to be spinning around him. He blinked his eyes hard, and when he could finally focus he realized he was inside a car! He saw the open window. No sweat, he thought, and sprang toward it. SMACK! He spiraled into the door. He shook himself off in disbelief. Something was not working right. He was getting ready to try again when suddenly the car came to a stop. The cricket froze, wondering what was going to happen next.

       *   *   *   *

Julie pulled up in front of a huge modern skyscraper. She looked out the window and up, up, up to the top floor. She was not looking forward to this meeting. She composed herself, took her valet parking ticket from the attendant, and got out of the car.

       *   *   *   *

Yes! She left the window open! The little cricket tried to escape again, but again he torpedoed into the door. Dazed and startled, he began to panic. Then he felt it, the strange numbness behind him. He turned and looked over his wing. He stared at himself in horror. One of his powerful jumping legs had been torn off. His most valuable defense was gone. Terror descended on him, and he dragged himself to the first available cover. He sat motionless in the dark beneath the driver's seat.

       *   *   *   *

In David Brown's office, Julie's face was flushed with apprehension. Julie had a hard time looking at this man. "I didn't mean to create such a problem," she apologized.

David was impatient. "I know this is difficult for you, Julie, that's why you should let me handle everything. Then you won't have to trouble yourself over things that are too complicated for you. I've chosen Viveca Smothers to do the rewrites. I'm sure she can handle it."

"Tony didn't particularly like her work, you must have known that. I don't think he'd want her to finish something of his."

"This is business, Julie. MoonStone paid Tony a lot of money for this book and they want their product. It's not a matter of what Tony might or might not want. You've read the manuscript; there are problems. It has to be dealt with."

Julie's composure was starting to crack. "I don't think it's right for someone else to finish his work."

David stood and walked around the desk to where she was seated. He knelt down beside her in much the same way an adult kneels beside a child they are trying to coax. He patted her hands, which were clasped in her lap. "Julie, come on now. You're not being realistic. There is a considerable sum of money at stake here. This is a legally binding contract I'm talking about." He turned the swivel chair toward him and placed his hands on either side of her, cupping them against her thighs. Julie stiffened, resentment flashing in her eyes. David went on, in that irritatingly patronizing way of his, "Sure, you could get out of the contract, but it would cost you the advance. You don't want to have to pay back the advance, now do you?"

Julie squirmed uncomfortably and then slid out of the chair to leave. "Tony used it as a down payment on the house, you know that."

David was immune to the subtlety of her rejection. His only real concern had been satisfied. He reached for the phone, and with his back to Julie dismissed her with, "I'll send you a copy of the galleys when Viv is done."

In the elevator, Julie was furious, then frightened, and then confused. She stared at the numbers above her, blinking each floor off as she descended. Tears threatened to overcome her, but she fought to hold them back.

*   *   *   *

The cricket was still on the car floor, beneath the steering wheel. He was staring upward, contemplating his predicament, when the car door suddenly whooshed open. Julie slid onto the seat. Her foot narrowly missed crushing him. He freaked, fell over himself, and then backed cautiously away from her shoe. He retreated under the seat again and then peeked upward. He didn't like her. He didn't like her at all.

*   *   *   *

Charles Jessup wore his bank manager title like it was his favorite suit. He liked being in charge, and he was deft at keeping the conversation focused on financing.

"Mrs. Maxwell, when you and your husband applied for the loan on the house we set up this payment to coincide with the balance of his publishing advance. We show here that we were to receive that amount two months ago."

"I know Mr. Jessup, but..." Julie struggled with her thoughts. "The book wasn't actually finished."

"Mrs. Maxwell, may I call you Julie?" Julie nodded her agreement. "Julie, foreclosure is a terribly unfortunate thing to have to consider. It has both immediate and very far-reaching consequences. Maybe there is someone who could help you with this payment?"

"Not really. My parents might be able to help out some, but the whole payment would be impossible. Is there any way I could pay part of it and have an extension on the rest?"

Mr. Jessup handed a stack of papers across the desk to Julie. "Maybe we could do some refinancing. Why don't we start with these credit applications?"

Julie stared anxiously at the papers. She was too embarrassed to volunteer that she had lost her job, and that every bill she and Tony had was now seriously in arrears. She looked at her lap, unable to look Mr. Jessup in the face.

"I'm sure once you fill these papers out and we are able to look at some other options it will all work out just fine."

Julie gathered up the papers and left with a barely audible, "Thank you."

*   *   *   *

In the car, the cricket was formulating a plan. Even though he couldn't jump he could still climb and crawl using his other legs. He could get up on her shoe and then climb up her pant leg and then onto the steering wheel and yes—upward and outward to freedom.

*   *   *   *

Julie burst into tears as she slid into the car. It seemed like it would never end. She hung over the steering wheel and sobbed from her heart, "I can't stand it. Oh God, I want you back!" She started the engine, snapped the radio off, and headed for the open highway. She fought to see the road through her tears. "I can't lose the house. I can't lose the house. I just can't!"

As the cricket sat listening to Julie crying above him, her sadness lessened his fear of her. Quietly, and ever so cautiously, he began his ascent.

The muted humming of the car engine began to calm Julie. She was glad it was a long ride home. She was more comfortable with her solitude when she was alone. The tears gradually dried on her cheeks. Suddenly, she was startled by something moving near her knee. Damn, she thought, it's that bug. There are too many bugs out here in the country. They're everywhere. It wouldn't be the first time one had flown in the window and taken a little nibble. It was that very fact that made Julie squirm again, trying to find whatever it was that had caught her eye. She was certain the little bugger would fly up her pant-leg and take a bite.

There was another movement, this time against her hand. She let out a little yelp and swerved the car by jerking the wheel. Night bugs seemed to have a more sinister nature than day bugs, and it was getting on towards night. Paranoia won out. Julie pulled off the road. She got out of the car and dusted herself off, shaking first one pant-leg and then the other. Then she leaned in the car and waved her hand in a shooing motion, peering in the nooks and crannies down by the gas pedal and along the floor. Nothing. Julie reassured herself that it, whatever it was, had taken its leave. She climbed back in the car and started the engine. The cricket, too frightened to move, was now clinging to the steering wheel.

Julie pulled the car back onto the highway and within moments she felt something brush against her hand again. Her heart stopped. She glanced down and saw the tiny prehistoric-looking little creature hanging on to the steering wheel for dear life. She raised her hand up instinctively in a swatting position.

"Hey, watch it!" screamed the little cricket. "Watch where you swing those fingers, lady. They're deadly weapons, you know."

Blinking her eyes and trying to focus, Julie looked at the little bug with disbelief. He was struggling to pull himself along the side of the steering wheel toward the top.

He looked up at her. "What are you staring at? Shouldn't you be watching where this death machine is going?"

Julie looked up just in time to miss an oncoming car. Driving while looking for a creature was one thing; driving while conversing with one was an entirely different matter. She jerked the wheel around and pulled off to the side of the road. The little cricket tumbled backwards down the wheel and nearly fell off. "Whoa! Now look what you have done. I have to start all over again!!"

Julie raised her hand to her face and checked for fever. "Maybe I'm coming down with something. God, I actually thought that bug said something to me."

"I most certainly am speaking to you. Who else is here? But I can't talk and climb at the same time." He gasped a little gasp as he started up the steering wheel again. "I'm going to the top where I can get a better look at you. And I'm not a bug! I'm a cricket. A Snowy Tree Cricket!"

Julie bent in close above him. "Get a better look at me?"

"Hey, could you please not breathe on me. The heat is stifling."

Julie sat up obediently, with a start. "Kind of a snooty little cricket." And then sarcastically, "I thought crickets were quick."

The cricket stopped climbing and looked up at her with the most dreadful look in his eyes. "I was, until you came along."

"Me?! What did I do?"

The cricket did not answer her, but continued his circumnavigation of the wheel with a very serious intent. Looking closely at him, Julie saw that he was actually quite cute. He was apple green and his eyes were like little dots of coal. His antennae sort of bobbed in time with his voice. His wings were beautiful lacey things; white and so delicate you could almost see through them. Then she noticed that he had four little legs, but only one long jumper. His little front legs were pulling him along, while the remaining strong one sort of pushed him from behind. Oh no, she realized, it was like trying to scale a mountain with only your hands and arms. "Poor little thing," she thought to herself. "What a drag," she said out loud.

"Precisely!" he said as he arrived topside. He positioned himself directly across from her and looked her right in the eye. "A drag is precisely what it is!"

Julie shook her head. "Who ARE you?"

"Ulysses, Ulysses O. Niveus."

"Pretty big name for such a little bug." Then she realized what she was doing. She collected herself, looked out the window hoping no one had seen this spectacle, and then reached for the ignition.

"That's right, Max, we had better get going. It's late, and I've been in this car all day."

Julie stared at him, dumbfounded. "How do you know my name?"

He ignored her question. "Well, now that you have come along and ripped my leg off, where else am I supposed to go? Do you know what would happen to me out there?" He looked out the window. "Now that I am like this...." He looked at the space where his leg used to be and shook his head in dismay.

Julie began to reel with confusion. "I ripped your leg off?"

"It was the car actually, but you were the one speeding down the road with absolutely no regard for anyone else that might be using it. I got clobbered by the rear view mirror and bounced in the window. If you want the gory details, my leg got left somewhere on the highway. Hell of a note, isn't it? A leg gone, just like that."

"Yes, a hell of a note."

"Look, we could sit here commiserating all night. Don't you have somewhere to go?"

Julie looked out the window and muttered to herself, "Commiserating?" She reached for the ignition again and started the car.

"There you go again! No consideration. I have to have a better place to ride than this. Every time you take a corner I about wind up on the floor again."

Julie wasn't sure she liked this little smart aleck. "Where would you like to ride?" And then muttering to herself again, "I must be losing my mind. Maybe this is what having a breakdown is like after all. It just creeps up on you, and then whammo—the funny farm."

Ulysses directed her toward the dashboard. "Over there, so I can see where we are going."

Julie stared at him for a minute, "Okay, the dashboard is fine."

He looked at her indignantly. "And how, pray tell, am I supposed to get myself over there? That leg? You remember the one. They call it a jumper. Get it? A jumper."

"Oh...." She raised her finger gingerly toward him.

"Closer please, that's right, up against the wheel. That's right." And he climbed on. Julie lifted him to the dash. He crawled off, walked up to the windshield and looked out.

As she headed for home, Julie had a heart-to-heart talk with herself. "Okay, Julie, you're talking to a cricket, a crippled cricket no less. This has gone a little too far. You've got a problem here, so...." She was determined to ignore him. But, it was amazing how real he seemed. How he seemed to know exactly what he wanted. And there was nothing wrong with having a vivid imagination. After all, isn't that what art is all about, imagination? And she is an artist, or was an artist. But this little fantasy seemed a bit more than imagination and didn't need to take hold. Maybe it would just go away.

Ulysses didn't say anything else either; he just sat looking out the window. When they pulled into the driveway, he turned and crawled to the edge of the dash. He looked imploringly up at her. Julie continued to ignore him, but as she got out of the car she weakened. She couldn't stand the way he was looking at her. She reluctantly raised her finger for him.

His look changed instantly from imploring to imperious. "Thank you. For a minute there I thought you were going to go off and leave me here."

He was so cute. She extended her finger toward him. "Oh God, I'm doing it again," she caught herself, "I'm believing this is happening."

At the prospect of her finger, Ulysses began to panic. "Where will I live? How will I survive?"

The light of a bright idea suddenly crossed Julie's mind and she urged him with her finger. He climbed on, head down, wings drooping, defeated. She made her way through the house to the deck. Unsure of what was happening, Ulysses sought refuge beneath the cuff of her sleeve.

Out on the deck, Julie said, "This might do."

Ulysses poked his little head out from under her sleeve and there before him were three perfectly wonderful old oak barrels overgrown with vegetables and weeds. He sprang from her hand and disappeared into the snow peas. Julie dropped to her knees and poked around in the leaves.

"What happened, where did you go?" She turned a leaf and there he was on his back, rocking furiously to and fro, trying to turn himself right side up. His 'little' legs were racing in midair. Julie reached her finger in and tipped him over, ever so gently. The painful reality of his predicament had been driven home. He looked sadly up at her, and retreated into the vines.

*   *   *   *

She couldn't sleep. She stood by the window, and stared out at the barrels in the moonlight. She listened to the crickets in the field. "It's lunacy," she thought to herself. "Crickets do not talk. He didn't really say anything." She contemplated the barrel a while longer. But there was something about him; something about the little guy, she just couldn't put her finger on it. She thought about that for a moment. As she climbed into bed she thought, "Good thing you didn't put your finger on it!" And that made her smile.

*   *   *   *

In the morning, Julie sat on the edge of her bed in her robe. She stared across the room at the open closet door. On a row of hooks hung several brightly colored smocks. They had stains and dusty splotches of clay on them. They were the clothes she had worked in. She crossed the room and fingered the fabric affectionately but with reserve. She had been a pottery teacher for a very long time.

In the kitchen, over her coffee, she looked around at the rest of her house. It was messy, uncared for. She noticed the mess in the same way she noticed her smocks, as if she hadn't seen it for a long, long time. "This can't go on forever," she thought, "I've got to pull myself together here."

Her eyes wandered to the barrels. He was such a preposterous bug. He sat on her knuckle like it was a throne, yet he was so vulnerable. She puzzled over that for a moment. He seemed so real. Maybe she had actually seen the cricket and it was only the conversation she imagined. But, hadn't he actually said his name? How could she have dreamed up a name like Ulysses O. Niveus? That did it. She went to the sliding glass door and opened it. She poked her head out and peered into the barrels.

"Hello?" she whispered tentatively, but there was no response. "Thank God." She breathed a little sigh of relief and went back in the house. Enough of this nonsense, she needed to get down to business. She began to clean and straighten and organize the house. But, no matter how busy she tried to be she couldn't stop herself from thinking about the cricket. She could relate to him, to his loss. It was a terrible thing to wake up one day and realize that your life would never be the same. Alone, for the first time, in a strange new house, in a strange new town—she knew that feeling that nothing was right, and she knew what it could do to you. No matter what anyone tried to do or say, nothing was right. "Poor Ulysses," she thought, "he has such a struggle ahead of him."

She went to the barrel again. "Are you all right?" She waited for an answer. Still nothing. She knelt beside the barrel and poked her fingers in the leaves. He was so easy to spot the night before. But now the branches, dirt and leaves looked like branches, dirt and leaves, instead of the haven they had created around him. "Oh well," she resigned herself, "I guess I imagined the whole thing." Julie went back in the house to try again to concentrate on her housekeeping.

Beautiful pieces of Julie's pottery decorated each room. She had a magnificent collection of frog figurines that she had sculpted from clay. As she dusted each piece, she explored it with her fingers, and a longing began to well up inside her. She diverted her thoughts to her plants. They were wilted and in desperate need of attention. She decided to move some of the large ones out onto the deck so she could hose them off. As she sprayed them with water, she just naturally gave the barrels a spritz too. Immediately she heard a squeaky little scream. Not wanting to believe her ears, Julie stepped back from the barrels.

In the barrel, a bedraggled, soaking wet Ulysses pulled himself out of the foliage and then onto the edge. Choking and coughing, he made his way around the barrel toward Julie.

Unable to ignore what she was seeing, Julie stopped watering her plants and said to him, "It's you. You *are* here."

"Where else would I be? What does it take for you to realize that I am stuck here and I am in a terrible fix? I don't need any more problems from you."

Julie went toward the barrel and knelt beside it. "I'm sorry, I didn't mean...I mean...I'm just having a little trouble believing you really happened."

Dragging his remaining, now drenched, leg behind him, Ulysses crawled away from her. "I'm having a little trouble believing this really happened myself, but every time I look at the air where my leg is supposed to be, I'm reminded."

Julie crawled alongside the barrel behind him. "Well, I didn't mean to...I didn't mean for this to happen."

"Mean to or not," he disappeared into the leaves, "here I am."

"Wait! Talk to me," Julie pleaded. "Tell me what you want."

"How can I?" he said from within the greenery, "when I don't know what I want." He thought about it for a second and then cried out, "I want my leg back!"

"Well, you can't have your leg back, unless you're one of those grow 'em back kind. Are you?"

"No!" he snapped. Then he peeked out of the barrel at her. "I'm never going to grow it back. Do you have any idea how long never is?" And he vanished again. Then she heard him muttering to himself. "I don't know what I want. I don't know what to do. It wasn't something I gave a lot of thought to, life without leg." He peeked out again. "How are you supposed to know what to do if you have never done it?" And then he was gone again.

Julie sat staring at the barrel, dumbfounded. "I know what you mean." She poked around in the leaves trying to find him, but he was gone. She caught herself and realized she was doing it again; she was talking to a cricket. She collapsed in a heap next to the barrel and held her head in her hands, "What is happening to me?"

*   *   *   *

In her bedroom, Julie stretched out on the bed and pulled a cold rag over her face. Maybe she could sleep it off. Maybe when she woke up she would find that it was just a dream, a weird little nagging dream. The sliding glass door was open, the breeze was dancing lightly through the leaves of the great tree and Julie was soon drifting into sleep.

From somewhere way off in the distance, she heard another squeaky little scream. She sat bolt upright on the bed and snatched the rag from her face. She looked out at the barrel. There was another scream. She tried to ignore it. But then came a more serious scream. She got up and rushed outside to the barrel.

Ulysses was hanging in a spider's web that was strung between the barrels and the deck. A huge black spider was circling him with webbing, and moving in for the kill. Julie gasped, and plucked the little cricket out. He was covered with sticky webbing. In her hand he was motionless. He looked dead. She gave her hand a jiggle, and then another. Ulysses finally responded with a little quiver of life.

He moaned.

Julie tried to pick the webbing off of him, but her fingers were too big.

Ulysses regained consciousness and was stunned when he looked up at her. "It's you! I might have known. What are you trying to do, finish me off?"

"What am I trying to do? I was just about to ask you the same thing." She set him down on the table and went for a pair of tweezers.

Ulysses was kicking and straining and sticking to himself. "Hey, wait a minute. You're not going to just go off and leave me like this are you?"

"No, I'm not going to leave you like this." She came back, tweezers in hand.

Ulysses shrieked with fright.

"Oh shush, would you," she said as she plucked a bit of webbing from his leg. "I'm not going to hurt you. What happened, anyway? Did you fall out of the barrel?"

"No! I dove out! I'm on my way back to Thomson's farm where I came from."

"Oh really? Well, my dear little friend, the Thomson place is fourteen miles from here. If you wanted to go back there, why didn't you just tell me? That would solve this little problem for both of us."

Julie continued plucking the sticky web off of him. She turned him onto his back to get the last little bits. He instinctively tried to turn himself right side up, but without the leverage of his other big leg he spun hopelessly around on his back.

Rocking back and forth, he got very upset. "Why should I tell you anything?" He began ranting in time with his rocking. "It's your fault I'm in this fix. It's your fault I'm stuck here!"

"Hey, wait a minute! I don't have to listen to this." She stepped back from the table and stared down at him, defiantly. "I'm trying to help you and you are totally ungrateful and rude."

"Rude? You come along and rip my leg off and you call me rude?"

Julie continued staring at him.

Frustrated, Ulysses stopped ranting and rocking and glared up at her. "Are you just going to stand there?"

"I might. As a matter of fact, yes, yes I am." She let him struggle for a minute longer while she considered what was happening. "Okay," she mused to herself, "first you thought you imagined him, now you are having an argument with him." She picked him up between her fingers and looked him in the eye. "I don't know who you are, Mr. Uppity Cricket, but this little fantasy is coming to an end!"

She grabbed her car keys and headed out the door, cricket in hand. When she got in the car she sort of tossed him onto the dashboard. "There! Your favorite spot." Ulysses moved across the dashboard in a huff.

Julie was concerned about herself, really concerned. She was speeding down the highway with incredible determination, and at the same time asking herself over and over, "Where are you going? What are you doing?"

The next thing she knew, she was crawling through the hedges that surrounded the Thomson farm. "I can't believe I'm doing this." She stopped for a minute and looked up. The beauty of the farm took her breath away. A grand old farmhouse. Gardens of flowers and herbs. Vegetables. Fruit trees. A husband. A wife and some kids. It was a perfect little paradise.

She opened her hand and looked at the little guy. "Will there be someone…something…here to help you?"

"I doubt it, they all think I've gone to that Great Headlight in the Sky. Just put me down over there," Ulysses directed her. "Over there by the trough."

Julie set him down and then felt a terrible pang of sadness.

"Okay," he snapped, "now scram!"

"Scram?"

"That's right! And thanks for everything!"

Julie started toward the hedges, but the curiosity of it all made her stop and watch for a minute. Seeing him in this setting he looked like any other insect in a flurry of barn flies. Except, in spite of all the fluttering and hopping about that the other bugs were doing, Ulysses just sat there, pathetically lopsided and confused.

One little cricket that looked almost exactly like Ulysses moved toward him and sort of nudged up against him. She appeared to be happy to see him. Then abruptly the little cricket backed away. Ulysses tried to hop toward her but faltered, stumbled…his wings fluttered and he made an odd little sound—almost a chirrup, but not quite. Julie couldn't believe her eyes.

All of a sudden, the man came out of the barn. All of the other insects disappeared in a flash. Julie ducked behind the woodpile. The man was carrying some buckets and heading for the trough. Ulysses spiraled into the air and disappeared.

Then Julie heard Ulysses cry out, "Max…. help me…."

As the man neared the trough, Ulysses was silenced. Julie gasped. She was horrified. What if the cricket had been crushed by the man's huge work boots? The man stooped to fill his buckets, and then Julie realized that the man was not aware of her or Ulysses. He didn't hear the little cricket's call for help. He was not at all aware of the drama she was caught up in.

Julie waited for a moment and then, as she crept toward the trough, she whispered, "Ulysses? Are you all right? Where are you?"

There was no response.

In a louder whisper, "For God's sake, if you're all right, say something."

Another long silence, and then she heard, "Over here, the bucket."

Julie rushed to the bucket and looked in.

"Not in the bucket, fool, down here!"

Julie peered over the top of the bucket and there he was, in a mess of mud—an imprint of the man's boot only a fraction of an inch from him. He was helplessly stuck on his back.

Julie was so relieved she found him. She smiled, "What you need are some wheels." She reached down and picked him up. He sputtered and choked. His voice cracked as he pleaded, "Please, take me away from here."

When she pulled into the driveway and got out of the car, her shoulder had a splotch of mud on it. A wee tiny voice from under her collar said, "The snow peas, please." Tears began streaming down her cheeks.

The dampness on her pillow awakened Julie from her nap. She was disoriented. It was hard to wake up. She looked out at the barrel and frowned. She got up and went to the window and stared at the barrel for a very long time. Then she realized she was late! She went into the bathroom and splashed cold water on her face and stared at herself in the mirror. It all seemed so real, and yet....

＊　　　　＊　　　　＊　　　　＊

Julie rushed through the small beach town. She hated being late. Slightly on edge, and out of breath, she hurried toward Ian and Annie's. She raced up to the door and knocked. Ian and Annie both greeted her. Annie took her coat and Ian gave her a big hug. "Where have you been?" Annie quizzed her, "I thought you were coming early."

Julie hugged Ian back. "It's a long story." As she looked over his shoulder she saw a man, about thirty-something, sitting in the living room. Julie shrank back from Ian's shoulder as John Williams rose out of his chair and started toward them. Julie looked pleadingly at Annie.

"That's our friend John," Annie reassured her. "He's up from the city for a few days."

"Why didn't you tell me?"

John approached Julie with his hand extended. "Julie, I've heard so much about you. I feel like I know you."

Julie shook his hand and smiled tentatively. She glared at Annie.

Annie was impervious. "Anyone for an appetizer? You guys go on in the living room, I'll get them."

Julie wasn't budging, "I'll help you, Ann."

In the kitchen, when they were safely out of earshot, Julie grabbed her friend's arm. "How could you?"

"How could I what? What's the matter?"

"I thought you understood."

"Understood what? What are you talking about?"

"This. This little soiree you've planned."

Annie laughed. "Planned? I didn't plan anything. John just showed up an hour ago. He and Ian have been friends since they were kids. They're like brothers. He just got separated and he's not doing so well."

That did it. "Separated? Oh God…" Julie reached for her coat and started to put it on.

Just then, Ian came through the door. "Where are the nibbles?" When he saw Julie with her coat half on he knew something was wrong.

"She's all upset," Annie told him, "because John is here. Will you please tell her this is not a big deal?" She looked at Julie, "Honestly, I had no idea you would react like this or I would have called you when he got here."

Ian shook his head "no" at Julie, and said reassuringly, "We wouldn't do something like that to you, kiddo. Annie's right, we didn't think this up, it just happened."

Julie felt a bit foolish. "Oh you guys, I'm sorry. I don't know what's wrong with me. I guess it's everything piling up."

Ian helped her take her coat off. "Relax, Jule. It's no big deal, okay?"

Unexpectedly, John entered the kitchen. "There must be something pretty special about these appetizers."

Everyone laughed, Julie nervously. She straightened herself and gave Annie a little hug. She felt awkward and self-conscious, but tried to appear calm.

*   *   *   *

At dinner, the conversation was mundane—news, weather, sports, the latest political scandal—until John asked, "Julie, you're an artist? A potter?"

Annie took the ball and ran with it, "A wonderful artist, that's one of her pieces over there." She pointed to a beautiful porcelain vase. A light, strategically placed, reflected through it, creating a glow that seemed to radiate from within. It was so delicately carved and brilliantly glazed that a magical three-dimensional world seemed to emerge from it.

John went on, "It's very beautiful. I've never seen anything quite like it."

Julie contemplated the vase for a moment before she spoke. "I did that one a long time ago, before my husband got sick." She dropped off into silence and stared at her plate.

After a long moment, John began to reveal himself. "I'm recently separated and I had no idea how difficult it was going to be. It's like a part of me, my arm or something, was suddenly torn off and now I'm faced with figuring out how to live without it." Julie looked up at him with a startled look on her face. He stopped and then, "I'm sorry if I've said something to upset you."

"No, it's not that, it's just that I found this little bug in my car. His leg had been torn off. Well, he collided with the rear view mirror and that's how his leg got ripped off. He is having a very hard time of it."

John, Ian and Annie all exchanged looks of concern and then stared at her. Annie spoke first. "Having a hard time of what?"

"Living without his leg. I put him in the barrels, but he's not happy about...it...at...." Julie noticed that they were all staring at her and then realized how strange her cricket story must sound to them. She was embarrassed and then flustered.

"John, I'm sorry, I didn't mean to compare you to a bug. I mean, I hadn't realized until just now how terrible Uly...I mean...."

They all continued staring at her. She pushed herself away from the table, rushed into the kitchen and gathered her things to leave.

Annie followed her and tried to stop her. "Don't go. This shouldn't be so hard Julie, you've got to start letting go."

"You don't understand, I can't let go."

"I'm worried about you, Julie"

"I know you are. Me too. You know that little cricket I just told you about? I actually thought I had a conversation with him."

Annie studied her friend with a look of grave concern. "But you know you didn't, right?"

"That's just it, I'm not sure."

Annie's face registered shock.

Julie went on, "I'm not sure of anything anymore. I mean I know he couldn't have said words, but it's like I can understand him or something. Annie, I feel like a one-legged cricket, my whole world has been torn apart."

*   *   *   *

On her way home, Julie thought about Ulysses and his dilemma. She wanted to believe that she had imagined the whole thing. It was too absurd to be real; not the bug himself, but the conversation—it was just too far out. She thought about how much like her little one-legged cricket she felt. She wanted to start over, but she didn't know where to begin.

Julie stopped at the crest of the hill and looked out at the ocean. The moon was rising in the night sky. It cast a great, long moonbeam across the water. For one lingering moment Julie stared wistfully at it. "Oh, Tony."

The wind gently caressing her hair was her response.

*   *   *   *

When she got home, she saw Ulysses sitting on the rim of the barrel. She opened the door to speak to him, but he disappeared. She stood beside the barrel and tried to find him. Every time she turned a leaf and revealed him he hurried toward the cover of another.

"Don't be afraid, Ulysses, I know how you feel." She poked her fingers around in the leaves, but he continued to elude her.

"Are you even real?" she asked into the barrel. She waited for an answer, but there wasn't one. And then, from out of nowhere, there he was, looking very cricket-like and saying nothing.

The sound of the field crickets swelled around the house. She looked up at the night sky emblazoned with starlight. "Night has a magical beauty out here, away from the glare of city neon," she thought to herself.

Caught in the mystery of the moment, she stood there listening for a long time. When she looked back in the barrel Ulysses was gone again.

As she turned out the deck lights and closed the door she said, as much to herself as to him, "I don't care if you are real or not, little friend, you and I have a lot in common. We are both going to have to learn to live again."

*   *   *   *

Every morning from then on when Julie opened her eyes she looked out the window and thought about the cricket's incredible struggle. She watched him when he didn't know she was watching. Just when he seemed ready to take a step toward accepting his new existence, something, some flashback of times past seemed to render him motionless. Then, at other times, it seemed like thoughts of leaping from branch to branch in the majestic old tree and matching wits with the wind were so vivid his nerves and muscles would tingle. Before he knew it he was in midair, feeling free, and forgetting. Then, that sickening twist, that nose-down, blood rushing feeling of descent and the crunch of wings against his spine. Betrayed again.

"What a fickle friend, memory," Julie thought, "forcing us to cling to the past and then driving us to reach and grasp for the future—stumbling, falling in the here and now." She could sense his confusion. And, she was beginning to grasp her own. Rallying between mad moments of despair and exhilarated moments of gratitude for still being alive tormented her. "As long as you are stuck in chaos and confusion," she thought, "you can't move forward." She became consumed with wanting to help him.

        *   *   *   *

She had a plan. What she needed now was information. A little drive to the university was in order. On her way out of town, Julie stopped at the post office. It was a rare occasion if you stopped at the Martin's Landing post office and found it empty. The old teller's window with the refurbished 50's style Formica counter, at the back of Lawson's store, was a favorite meeting place for everyone in town. You could grab a cup of coffee in the store on the way in, and know everything that was going on in town by the time you were on the way out. Today, Julie ran into Annie.

"I'm sorry about the other night," Julie told her friend. "I know I'm hard to deal with these days."

"It's okay, I understand," Annie reassured her. "But I do think you're spending too much time alone."

"I know you're worried, Annie, but I'm going to be fine, really." Then with a little tease in her voice, she added, "Besides, I'm not alone. I have my little friend Ulysses."

"Is this supposed to be some kind of joke?" Annie fired back.

"It's not a joke, I did find a cricket."

"Julie, what's happening to you? Are you getting weird? Imaginary friends are things we have when we're little. You know, you might need to talk to someone. It might help you start coping."

"It's not what's *happening* Annie, it's what *happened*. I'm finally beginning to realize what happened to me. I'm not getting weird. He's not imaginary. But what difference does it make whether I found a cricket or not?"

Annie was caught somewhere between concern and curiosity. She studied her friend and pondered for a moment what to say next.

Julie rifled through her mail. She recognized the handwriting on one of the envelopes and tore it open immediately. She pulled out a card with a photograph of an elegant piece of pottery on it.

"Danny...."

Annie, the eternal hopeful, asked, "Who's Danny?"

"He was one of my first students. He was really special. We've always sort of stayed in touch." Julie hurriedly read the note inside. "Wow, he is doing very well. He just opened a pottery supply shop in Marin."

Annie reached out and touched Julie's arm. "Any time you're ready to open your studio again I'm good for a little spit-shine and polish. You know that, don't you?"

"Yes, I know. And I appreciate the offer, but I'm not ready to go back to work yet. I'm going out to the university library today to do a little research on crickets. Want to come along for the ride?"

Annie just shook her head and then opened her P.O. Box and pulled out her mail. "Can't, Jule, I'm on call."

*   *   *   *

When Julie pulled into the campus parking lot she could tell it was between classes. There were hundreds of students scurrying about. She thought about teaching. She liked working with college art students. They were stimulating, excited about expressing themselves, expressing their ideas through their art. For a moment she believed she could start teaching again. Then she remembered when she met Tony. A rush of memories flooded her mind. As she got out of the car and crossed the campus, she felt lost without him.

"That's it," she realized to herself, "I got lost in we-land. When you love someone, and live with him for a long time, you forget your *self*." She thought about how her career was always being interrupted so his could be nurtured. "I wonder if I would have held on more tightly to myself if I had known." That thought surprised her. "God, am I bitter?" she questioned herself. "I can't be, we had a plan. We did."

She felt awkward thinking so much about herself. Selfish, self-indulgent. "But it isn't selfish," she contradicted herself, "or self-indulgent. It's, it's survival."

As she entered the library and its hush, she silenced her mental debate. She stared at the aisles and aisles of books. She couldn't remember why she was there. She had to walk herself back through her day in order to remember. She had almost forgotten that it was because of that little creep the cricket.

She searched the aisles and then sat down at a table with several books on insects strewn out in front of her. She searched through them looking for crickets. She found a picture that looked exactly like Ulysses. Beneath it was printed OECANTHUS NIVEUS: Snowy Tree Cricket.

"Oh my God, oecanthus niveus—Ulysses O. Niveus...."

*   *   *   *

As soon as she got home from the university, she went straight out to the deck and knelt beside the barrels, "Okay, Mr. Oecanthus Niveus, come out of there."

Nothing. No response.

"Come out of there!" she insisted.

Ulysses came meandering around the edge of the barrel from behind her. "Out of where?"

Startled, Julie turned toward him. "You are a Snowy Tree Cricket!"

"Well, thank you very much for that. It's reassuring to know that I know who I am."

"I went to the library today and read some books on insects." She leaned in close and really inspected him. She kind of pointed to his little legs and body. "What a finely tuned little creature you are, all air pipes and tympanic membranes."

Ulysses recoiled from her inspection. "Was! What a finely tuned cricket I was!"

"Ulysses, you could still have a wonderful life. You can still sing and fly and..."

"Jump? Certainly you weren't going to say jump!" He turned toward the cover of the vines, but Julie stopped him with the tip of her finger.

"You don't need that leg, you know the one, the jumper…for flying!"

"Who asked you anyway? I don't care what you think I need or don't need. What I don't need is your opinion about every little thing. I don't care what those books said. Who wrote them? Not crickets! And speaking of air pipes and tympanics, did those books tell you about water and mud and what happens to crickets that can't jump?"

"No."

"See there, you don't know the first thing about crickets." Ulysses and Julie stared at each other for a moment, and then he went on, "Winter is hard on the horizon, Maxwell. Did those books tell you what I'm going to do about that?"

Julie looked out to the ocean. The horizon was crisp and distinct and there wasn't a cloud in the clear blue sky. "It doesn't look like winter to me."

"My life depends on knowing. It's coming early this year, and it's going to be miserably cold and wet." He maneuvered around her finger and disappeared into the vines. "This barrel will get muddy. The vines will die, and I won't be able to get around. If I fall into the mud," his voice cracked with fear, "I'll…I'll…."

Julie realized, "You'll drown. If you get stuck in a puddle, you'll drown."

Ulysses poked his head out from under a leaf and nodded.

Julie went on, "So, what you are telling me is you need a new place to live."

Ulysses nodded again.

"Well, you could move inside," she gestured toward the open door, "and live in the fern."

Ulysses shuddered at the suggestion.

"Or you could fly south for the winter."

"Verrrrrry funny! Everything's a big joke to you." He disappeared again.

"Actually, I don't think it's funny at all."

"Leave me alone!"

"Okay, okay, so you need a new place to live."

Silence

"Right?"

Ulysses was mistrustful, "Right...."

"And you're not too keen on indoor living?"

"Right...."

Julie sat down beside the barrel and stared up at the tree.

Ulysses peeked out and saw her contemplating the tree. "Wait a minute," he panicked. "Wait just a minute. I'm not going up in that tree."

Julie was barely paying attention to him. She got up and went over to the tree and broke off the tips of a few dead branches. She set them down beside the barrel and went into the house.

Ulysses began pacing along the rim of the barrel with his pathetic little limp, and bemoaning his fate. "I'm not going up in that tree. It's positively out of the question. I'd blow away in a second. Bye-bye, Ulysses."

He was still complaining when Julie came back out to the barrel and started fiddling with the branches. "Oh hush for a minute, will you?"

She snipped, clipped, tied and glued bits and pieces of branch together until there was in her hand a tiny twig house. On four little posts there was a kind of miniature Robinson Crusoe with a ramp leading to a doorway. She held it up and examined it with pride.

"Well," she said to herself, "this is the most creative thing you've done in awhile." She reflected on that. It felt pretty good. She set the tiny twig house down, secured it in the barrel and then gave it a little shake with her fingers. "Yep, good and sturdy." She beamed proudly at Ulysses, "Pretty nifty, eh?"

"There are no words for it."

"Well, it's not the farm, but..."

At the mention of the farm, Ulysses saddened. Head down, hindquarter dragging, he pulled himself along the ramp to his new home. "It's unnatural," he muttered, and then disappeared inside.

Julie looked out beyond the deck to her deserted studio. She felt drawn to it. She got up and went out to it. She wiped a circle clean in one of the windowpanes and looked in. A crushed mound of clay sat dried and cracked on the wheel. Covered with dust, solemn rows of porcelain forms lined the shelves. It was a dismal picture compared to the enchanted studio she and Tony had so enthusiastically created. As she stood there, unable to open the door, her heart sank. "Tragedy," she thought to herself, "tragedy immobilizes you."

*   *   *   *

Retreating to her favorite spot in the living room, Julie propped the card she received from Danny strategically above her on the back of the sofa. She stared at it intently. Her deep thoughts were soon interrupted by an odd little sound. She sat up and took notice of the sound. Then after a moment she heard it again.

She looked out at the barrel. Ulysses was sitting on his little ramp and trying to position himself against the angle of it so he could rub his wings together and sing. Other crickets in the field were just beginning to signal the onset of night. Ulysses was failing miserably and becoming very frustrated. Julie got up and went to him, but as she drew closer he instinctively vaulted into the air and landed on his back at her feet. Stuck.

"I don't know what possesses me to think I can still do that," he complained. "One of these days I'll probably hurl myself into the wind and that will be that. I'll never be heard from again. Good riddance, good-for-nothing-cricket. Good riddance."

Julie reached down and tipped him right side up. He started toward the open door doing that little leap, hop, drag that tugged at her heart.

"Want a ride?" She put her finger down for him to get on.

As they entered the living room, Ulysses SHRIEKED out a SCREAM. He started frantically trying to make his way across Julie's hand toward her sleeve. He struggled as fast as he could but her sleeve was rolled up to her elbow. Julie's eyes darted around the room searching for what he was so afraid of.

"What is it? What are you so afraid of?"

"Raise your arm! Raise your arm!" he implored her.

Julie raised her arm to a horizontal position making it easier for him to get to her sleeve.

"What's the matter with you? What in the world are you so terrified of?"

Nearly exhausted, he finally made it to her sleeve. As he ducked for cover, he heaved, "The frogs!"

Julie looked around and saw her clay frogs through new eyes.

"Do you know what frogs do with crickets?" Ulysses shouted. "THEY EAT THEM!"

"Oh Ulysses, they aren't real. They are made of clay. I made them." The silence beneath her sleeve was deafening. She pushed on, "Did you hear me? I said...."

"I heard you!" He crawled slowly, and with as much nonchalance as he could muster, out from under her sleeve. He was very embarrassed but trying very hard not to show it.

Julie wanted to giggle. "I'm sorry you were so frightened. Is there anything I can do?"

Ulysses shook his head, "No, no, no." As he maneuvered back toward her finger, he surveyed the frogs one by one. "That one, I'd like to sit right on that one's big ugly head."

Julie smiled at the new courage in his voice. She set him down on a frog that was next to a photo of Tony flying his kite, and then sat down in a chair next to him. Her fingers gravitated toward the frog and she unconsciously began tracing the contours of its clay body. She pondered Tony's image for a moment and then, "Ulysses, where did you come from?"

"I came from the farm."

"No, where did you really come from? You can talk."

"All crickets can talk."

She glared at him for a second. He did not respond. She stared harder, more insistently.

Finally, he responded, "Maybe it's not what I say that's important, Max."

Her brow furrowed.

"Maybe it's what you can hear."

That startled her. She thought about what he had just said.

Ulysses went on. "I miss my life so much."

"I know what you mean."

"I was the fastest, farthest jumpinest cricket around, and now look at me. I'm afraid of clay frogs."

"But you can still fly and you can still sing. Why, with a little practice I just know you can still..."

"Don't say it! Look at me, I only have one leg."

"I am looking at you," she pointed at him and teased, "and actually you have five legs...one, two, three, four, five."

"Everything's a big joke to you. And what makes you think you know so much about crickets? Just because you read a few books, now you think you're an expert? I said I can't, and I can't!"

"Won't! You aren't as bad off as you think you are. There is a whole world still out there for you. But damn, you're going to have to stop feeling sorry for yourself before..."

Before she could finish her sentence Ulysses stopped her. "You know your pie-in-the-sky attitude makes me sick. I'm the one-legged cricket around here! You don't understand the first thing about what I'm going through." He started his trek down the back of the frog. "Take me out to the barrel."

"You know what? I understand plenty. But you are so busy feeling sorry for yourself, you don't even know what's going on around you."

Ulysses gave her a quick once-over. "I see you have all of your arms and legs!"

"Arms and legs aren't the only things you can lose." She looked at the picture of her husband and began to feel sick to her stomach.

"Oh yeah, and how do you know so much? What terrrrrible..."

"You listen to me, Mr. Uppity Cricket."

"Ulysses, that's Ulysses O. Niveus."

"I don't know who you are, and I don't know why you are here, but I have been trying to make your life a little easier since the accident."

"Which, by the way, was your fault, Miss Do-Gooder-Goody."

"No, it was not my fault. It was an accident. You were the one whizzing across the road not looking where you were going."

"It's all relative, don't you think?"

Julie rose from where she was seated and picked Ulysses up between her fingers. A large lump had formed in her throat and she had trouble speaking. "Yes. It is all relative. Do you know what a widow is?"

"Yeah, it's a big spider."

"I'm a widow! My husband is dead." She pointed to the picture of Tony. "I lost him forever!" She grabbed Ulysses in her hand, took him out to the barrel and tossed him in. He rolled into the dirt, but landed right side up. He stared up at her.

"I'm a widow, Ulysses," she cried as she stormed back into the house and slammed the door. She threw herself onto the sofa and sobbed, "I'm a widow, I'm a widow, I'm a widow...I'm a widow."

*   *   *   *

When she awakened, Julie's eyes struggled to focus on the first images of the day. Hesitantly, they adjusted themselves to the light. Then, momentarily, she sank back into oblivion. She unconsciously rolled over and stretched. She nearly fell off the couch. It startled her.

Opening her eyes, Julie looked up at the picture of Tony on the end table. She reached out and touched it. "Widow," she whispered. She hadn't said it even once since Tony died. It seemed that for as long as she didn't say it, it wasn't true. Now that she had actually said it, she felt relieved, like mouthing the word had released some huge pressure from within her. It was the first morning in a long, long time that she hadn't had to fight back the sadness. It wasn't gone, but somehow now she was out of the past and into the present—into the real world. She looked out the window at the barrel and then chided herself, "Right Julie, you're in the real world all right."

She rolled over onto her back and let her thoughts drift back to Tony again. She wished they had moved sooner, instead of postponing it because Tony didn't think they were ready. It irritated her a little when she remembered how many things Tony had decided for them both, how often she had given things up that she really wanted because he said it wasn't time, or it wasn't right for them.

Then she remembered what he said at the end, about never allowing the things she really wanted to slip away from her. She had almost forgotten that conversation, or had blocked it out. He told her, "Now, Julie. Do the things you always wanted to do. Don't let anything hold you back ever again. Dare to be what you always wanted to be—what you were meant to be."

It was almost as if he was apologizing for their life. At the time, she couldn't hear him. She rejected what he said completely, she was so totally overcome by fear of life without him. How strange it was that now, now she could hear his words so clearly.

She saw the card from Danny still perched on the back of the sofa and took it in her hand. Almost immediately she set it down again. Entertaining thoughts about her future was not going to be easy. It's rather like waking up in the morning, she thought, when sensations first begin to tingle and your eyes are just starting to focus on the first images of the day. Hesitantly at first, she reminded herself, they adjust themselves to the light. Blinking, coming up to consciousness, then blinking, sinking, down into oblivion again. "Yes, yes," she thought, "not to be afraid Julie, it's a lot like waking up."

The phone rang. She answered. It was the bank. She had to be there by three.

*   *   *   *

Just as she was about to leave, she saw Ulysses perched on top of his house looking in the window for her. Julie poked her head out the door. "Good morning," she said politely, and a little apologetically.

"And what are you all in a flurry about this morning?"

"Am I all in a flurry?" She was surprised. "I have to go out and I can't be late." She pulled back from the doorway.

"Where are you going?"

She stuck her head back out the door. "I have important business at the bank and I'm going to stop and see an old friend on the way."

"Define friend." Ulysses started down the roof of his little hut away from her. He mumbled, "I might like to come along for a ride, you know. Instead of being left behind in this barrel all by myself. Did you ever think of that?"

"Well, no, I hadn't. But today's not a good day. Can I get you anything before I leave?"

"How about a leg for starters?" he snapped, and disappeared into his house.

"Ulysses, I didn't deserve that."

*   *   *   *

The pottery supply shop was actually a converted garage. Outside was a hand painted sign that read THE POTTER'S WHEEL. Julie sat in the car for a minute contemplating what she was about to do.

From under her collar, "You sure talk big."

Julie rolled her eyes, got out of the car and entered the store guardedly. She was both excited to be seeing her old friend and apprehensive about being so close to the work she had loved so much. The shop was small and filled with everything a potter could need, or want. A showcase of pottery ran along the length of one wall. Each piece was labeled with the potter's name and the date the work was done. Julie stopped and looked in at some of hers. They stood out from all the rest.

She went up to the counter and listened for a moment to the humming of the potter's wheel emanating from the curtained doorway. On the counter was a bell with a sign that said PLEASE RING FOR SERVICE. She wanted to ring, but she waited, not wanting to interrupt the potter who was so hard at work.

The wheel stopped suddenly and she heard "Shit!" exclaimed from behind the curtain.

Julie chuckled, knowing all too well what that meant. She rang the bell. Danny Campbell, a burly, bear-hug kind of guy, bearded and covered with clay, burst through the curtain. It took him a few seconds to realize who it was that was standing in front of him. Finally, "Julie! God, it's you!" He ran around the counter and gave her a big hug. "You got my card. Where have you been?"

Julie hugged him back. "Danny, it's so good to see you." The hug felt so warm to her. "How are you? The store looks great."

But Danny wanted to know why he hadn't seen her. "Where have you been?"

"Didn't you hear? Tony died last year. Cancer."

Danny was taken aback. "No... Julie... I'm sorry."

"We moved out to the beach just before he got sick. I finally got my own studio. It was wonderful, and then wham. It happened so fast."

Danny was awkwardly silent, wanting to comfort his friend but not knowing how. "God, what can I say to her," he thought to himself. He searched her eyes hoping to find a clue there. But there wasn't one. Julie eased his discomfort by moving away from him and perusing the aisles. Danny followed behind her as she continued to talk. "I haven't been on the wheel for over a year, Danny. I went back to teaching right away, but it's hard to teach when you can't work. Know what I mean?" She stopped to admire an exquisitely shaped tea bowl. The crackled glazed perfectly accented its shape. She touched it. "This is nice, Danny. Real nice."

"Yeah, I finally got into raku."

Julie smiled. She had always known that raku would become his passion, once he got beyond his fear.

"I'm experimenting with some new formulas right now," Danny went on. "I'm getting ready for the show at Zachariah's. I thought maybe I'd be seeing you there. I couldn't believe it when he accepted my work." Danny went to the counter and retrieved some papers he promptly handed to Julie. "These are the applications. Zack Thomas would flip if he ever saw your work, Jule. Why don't you call him? It might be a good way for you to...."

"I can't get up for it, you know. I'm all blocked inside. Sometimes I think I'll never..."

Danny took her hands in his, "You can't let these go to waste, Julie. Never is a long time." A bell suddenly went off and immediately diverted Danny's attention. "I'm firing. Want to check the cones with me?"

Outside, Julie stood close behind Danny as he put on his welder's glasses and big asbestos mitts. The roar and hiss of the gas jets filling the kiln with fire excited her. As he un-bricked the opening and exposed the white-hot interior filled with pottery, Julie's face flushed with the fire glow. Her breathing quickened. Her eyes reflected the excitement she was experiencing. She was being seduced by the fire.

"You have some fabulous pots in there, Danny."

"I had a great teacher."

*   *   *   *

It was a good visit. It brought her close to the water without actually throwing her in. Julie and Danny were just about to say good-bye when Ulysses came out from under her collar and perched himself boldly on her shoulder. He looked right at Danny.

Danny bent in to inspect Ulysses. "Hey, who is this little guy?"

Julie pulled back in embarrassment, "Oh God." She was mortified. "I found him, or he found me, I don't know which." Then she noticed that Ulysses was staring right at Danny. "He must like you, Danny. He's very particular about the company he keeps. He only has...."

"One leg!" Danny exclaimed. "I'd take really good care of him if I were you." Danny went over to a bookcase where all of his art books were shelved. He searched for something specific. "Here it is. In China crickets are revered, Jule. They are good omens, you know, like for wealth and success. They live in these little clay houses the potters make for them."

"Are you kidding? Let me see those." Julie could hardly believe her eyes. She looked down at Ulysses who she could swear was giving her a "lucky you" kind of glance. It made her laugh.

*   *   *   *

The bank was not such a happy encounter. Mr. Jessup would like to have been telling Julie better news, but he had no choice. "I'm afraid we have a much more serious problem here than I first expected, Julie. The bank does not want to refinance you. You aren't working and your financial obligations are in drastic circumstances."

"But what about the money my parents are willing to give me?"

Charles Jessup liked Julie, and he felt for her circumstances, but he didn't want to see her get in any deeper than she already was. "Julie, let me be very frank with you," he said almost paternally. "I don't think you are capable of holding on here. There would be more options open to you if you had an income."

"I have to be able to keep the house. Couldn't you give me just a little more time? I know I can get back to work, I just need a little more time. Please. Please, Mr. Jessup."

Unable to turn her down, he temporarily put aside his better judgment and gave in. "Well, I could put this on hold for sixty days, but at the end of that time the foreclosure will begin if you haven't made the payment. And Julie, the machinery is impossible to stop once it is set in motion."

*   *   *   *

At home, Julie and Ulysses pored over the application papers from Zachariah's Art Gallery. She looked at Ulysses. He looked back with an encouraging, "Why not?" She went to the phone and dialed.

*   *   *   *

Julie's studio reflected the death of her artistic spirit. Once supple and cool balls of clay were now dried out and hard like rocks. An open container of glaze was caked and cracked like an old riverbed. Her tools were a mess. Julie moved hesitantly toward the shelves where the finished pottery stood.

Ulysses was on her shoulder. "Yuck, it looks like something died in here."

She dusted off some pots and lined them up in front of her. "Something did die," she touched her hand to her heart, "in here."

She looked over her work and was surprised at how much there was. Some of the pieces were perfect, and some of them looked like they had been thrown by a child. She lingered over them. "This is like a history of my life." Then she held up a dull, misshapen pot. "This is the work I tried to do when Tony was sick. Out of balance, lifeless." She held up a piece that fairly breathed with life. She carefully ran her fingers over it, exploring, examining, feeling every aspect of it. "I did this at a much happier time. What a difference."

She moved to the wheel and the crushed mound of clay, a glaring reminder of her last days in the shop. She sat down and placed her hands on it. She "stepped back in time" for a moment. She could feel Tony's hands on hers. A lone tear strayed across her cheek.

Ulysses piped up, "You have a gift, Max...."

Lost in her memory, Julie was startled that Ulysses was saying the exact words that Tony had just spoken in her mind. She looked at the cricket in awe.

Ulysses went on, gently, "You miss him awfully, don't you?"

"I do, Ulysses. I want him here. I want to touch him and tell him how much I miss him."

"He knows," the little cricket said knowingly. Julie stared at Ulysses for a moment, believing him. "This is about you, Julie," he went on. "You have to try to be happy so you can be the artist you always wanted to be."

Julie was dumbfounded. "How...."

"Never mind, Maxwell, never mind." He looked exaggeratedly around the room. "Don't you have a lot to do before you meet Mr. Zachary Thomas?"

Zachary Thomas. Reality. Julie didn't want to go there. And then, almost defiantly, she retorted, "Not really. There is a lot of work here already."

Ulysses looked at her with disappointment. She rebuffed him by ignoring the look. She began polishing and packing up what was there. Ulysses shook his little head in dismay.

Julie tried to convince him, and herself, "Really, there is enough here to show him. Way more than I expected." She felt a little guilty, but not guilty enough to risk sitting down at the wheel. "Besides, there isn't time to do anything new. He wants to see these right away."

✳   ✳   ✳   ✳

Julie pulled up in front of the gallery and parked in the loading zone. She stared out at the two story plate-glass window that fronted it. Zachariah's was an intimidating art gallery. Ulysses was on the dashboard. He stared out at the gallery too.

Julie wanted to turn around and go home. "I don't want to do this. I don't want to do this at all."

"What?" Ulysses snapped. "What's the matter with you? Of course you want to do this!"

She reached for the ignition. "No, I don't think this was a good idea after all."

"Stop! He's expecting you for crying out loud."

"That's exactly what I feel like doing, crying out loud."

"Don't be ridiculous," Ulysses challenged her.

She took a deep breath, mustered up some courage and started to get out of the car.

"Hey, what about me?"

"But what if he sees you? He'll think I'm crazy. Of course, I *am* crazy."

Ulysses stared her down. As she raised him to her shoulder and he ducked out of sight, he promised. "Don't worry, I'll be very discreet."

Inside, the gallery was elegant, tasteful, and diverse. It was everything Julie had ever dreamed of achieving. She was very nervous as Zachary Thomas crossed the room to greet her. He was tall and handsome, so handsome it took her breath away. He had about him the air of confidence of a man who had definitely "arrived."

"Is there something I can help you with?" he asked.

"I have an appointment with Mr. Thomas."

"You must be Julie. I'm Zack. It's good to meet you. You brought some of your work?"

"Yes, it's in the car."

"I'll send someone out to help you. Why don't we do this in my office, upstairs."

In his enormous loft office, on an imposing and ornate mahogany table that had a mirror-like shine, Julie unpacked her boxes. She carefully unwrapped each piece and displayed it for Zack. Her heart was pounding so hard she had trouble catching her breath. She had brought the best she had to offer.

Zack stepped back from the table and stood looking at her work. He walked slowly around the table and examined it all very carefully. He did not speak for what seemed like an interminably long time.

And then finally he said, "Julie, you're very talented, very talented indeed." He picked up one of the pieces. "I haven't seen work as exciting and original as yours in a long time. This is done in the tradition of the great Chinese masters." He looked at Julie with very pointed interest. "Tell me, Julie Maxwell, where have you been hiding yourself?"

*   *   *   *

As Julie was getting ready to leave the gallery, Zack stopped to speak with a customer. Ulysses was so excited he could not contain himself so he came out onto her shoulder. Julie freaked. "What are you doing?! Get back under my collar this minute."

"Julie, you're like the fastest, farthest jumpinest cricket of clay."

As Zack approached, he swatted at Julie's shoulder and narrowly missed dashing Ulysses to the ground. The cricket ducked out of sight. Julie was completely taken aback.

Zack tried to allay her fears. "It was nothing, just a fly."

Julie, knowing full well what it was, hurried toward the exit. "I'll have some more pots ready for you in a couple of weeks, Zack. I can't tell you how much I appreciate...how grateful I am." She extended her hand toward him, but he brushed past it and embraced her with a slightly more than friendly hug. It caught her totally off guard. And, he didn't let go, at least not right away.

"I'm the one who's grateful, Julie. I think you and I are going to have a long and happy relationship."

*　　　　*　　　　*　　　　*

Outside, Ulysses was all in a dither. "A fly!?? That guy's a real creep. I could be squashed on your shirt right now! I don't like him at all!"

"Calm down. You aren't squashed on my shirt right now. You're fine. Serves you right anyway, Mr. Don't Worry I'll Be Discreet."

"He's quick to use his weapons. That's not a good sign. Did he even give one thought to the life he could be ending?" Ulysses eye-balled her but continued on, not waiting for an answer, "No, he did not!"

"Oh, Ulysses, Zack is a very nice man. You'll see."

*　　　　*　　　　*　　　　*

Julie was thrilled about her new opportunity. She couldn't wait to share the news with her mother. She called her right away.

"Mom? Are you sitting down? Yes, today was the day. He loved my work. I'm going to be featured at the show. Can you believe it?! ...Mom. ...Mom. ...This is a job. It is work.... Yes, I can invite whoever I want. No, don't tell Margaret just yet. I know she's Tony's mother, Mom. I have to go down to see Zack again in a couple of weeks; I'll have lunch with her then. Mom, this is the first breath I've taken in my life without him...."

Julie hung up the phone. The glow was almost gone. She had been staying away from Tony's family for a reason. Her own pain had been more than she could bear.

*   *   *   *

The show at Zachariah's meant that the cleanup had to take place. Julie and Annie scrubbed, scraped, dusted and polished everything in the studio. Ian carted the trash away in his truck. As they worked, the studio began to come alive again. The wedging table was cleared off, the wheel was clean and ready to go, Julie's carving tools were lined up in neat little rows and her smocks were washed and hung up to dry. When they were finished, they all noticed how the whole studio just seemed to beckon for Julie to begin working.

"Now, if I can just DO something in here."

"According to the bank, you better," Annie chided her.

Julie nodded 'that's for sure,' and then said, "Let's eat."

On the deck, she hovered over the barbecue and tried to start it. Ian gravitated toward the barrels and stood over Ulysses' twig house. "Where is that little friend of yours?" He knelt down and tried to poke his fingers in the tiny doorway of the cricket's home.

"Be careful," Julie reprimanded him, "you might upset him."

Annie frowned. "Upset him?"

Ian retracted his hand and looked up at Julie with concern. "You're serious?"

"I tried to tell you, she's real serious," Annie chimed in.

In a very paternal tone, Ian said, "Julie, don't you think this cricket-thing has gone far enough?"

Julie was amazed. "Cricket-thing? I can't believe you guys still think I'm putting you on." She knelt beside the barrel. "Ulysses?"

Ian and Annie exchanged one of those "dubious" looks.

"Ulysses," she said into the foliage, "come out here. I want Ian and Annie to meet you."

Ian couldn't stand it. "You're talking to him like he can understand you. I mean even if there was a cricket...."

"There is a cricket." Julie lifted a leaf and there he was. "Right there."

Ian was shocked. Then Annie looked in. She stepped back. "What a weird looking little thing. He's so spindly. I thought crickets looked like beetles, sort of stubby or squatty or something."

Ian inspected him more closely, "He does have only one jumping leg." He tried to reach in and grab the cricket, but Ulysses disappeared in a flash. Ian and Annie were both startled by this.

"Dammit Ian, you frightened him! I told you he is very sensitive. Ever since the accident he is afraid of everything. Imagine how vulnerable he feels."

"Bugs don't feel, Julie."

"How do you know that, Ian?"

He thought about that for a minute and then laughed. "Oh Julie, you just feel sorry for him. Annie, you know how she is. This is just like that crazy cat. You remember, the one that fell out of the tree."

That satisfied Annie, sort of, but it was an awkward and strange moment for them all.

*   *   *   *

In the kitchen, later, Annie and Julie were making a salad while Ian tended to the barbecue outside. Julie could tell Annie wanted to say something.

Julie started peeling a cucumber and then decided to challenge her friend to speak up. "Well?"

Annie went to the sink and started washing the lettuce. She deflected Julie's question with a "Well what?"

"I know you have something you want to say Ann, I can feel it."

After a few false starts, Annie finally mustered up the courage to say what she had been thinking all night, "I'd just think you'd rather spend time talking to someone like John than this little cricket of yours."

Julie stopped peeling the cucumber and looked intently at her friend.

"But I wouldn't rather, Annie."

Annie stopped washing the lettuce and turned to face Julie. "How do you know you wouldn't rather? How do you know anything anymore, you are spending all of your time alone."

"Loneliness is not the enemy here, Annie. I was so young when I married Tony, I've never really been on my own." Julie grabbed a knife out of the drawer and began slicing the cucumber. "It's kind of like being in the driver's seat after being a passenger all my life."

Annie didn't know quite what to think of that. It was unsettling to her. She was opening and closing the cupboards in her search for the lettuce spinner, but she wasn't really paying attention to what she was doing. "I thought you were happy with Tony."

"I was. It's just so different now, with him gone. I feel like I'm on some sort of expedition. You know, kind of exploring who I am."

Annie and Julie were quiet for a moment. Annie finally stopped searching for the spinner and looked at Julie. "Aren't you afraid?"

"Of myself?" Julie thought about that for a minute. "I don't want to be. Not anymore. Besides, I don't think I have a choice, now do I?"

*　　　*　　　*　　　*

The morning was crisp and cool. Julie was standing outside her studio. Ulysses was on her shoulder. As she looked in the window, her face brightened with anticipation. She glanced at the cricket on her shoulder and he encouraged her with a nod. She opened the door and stepped inside. The sun was streaming in the window and there was a magical feeling all around her. Julie felt very alive, and kind of brand new.

She looked at Ulysses again and for a second she was taken aback. "Are you smiling at me," she asked him. "Is that a smile I see?"

Lost in the moment, she moved slowly around the shop, immersing herself in it. Without even having to look at what she was doing she reached across the wedging table and flipped a switch. Her breath quickened as the room filled with the sound of the humming of her wheel.

*   *   *   *

By late afternoon, it had become apparent that Julie had only been dabbling with her work all day. She had been tentative, playing with the clay, throwing "Dick and Jane" forms and not really challenging herself. She felt like she was getting into a swimming pool again for the first time after nearly drowning. Now it was time to get down to business.

She placed a large mirror directly in front of her wheel and then sat down and watched the reflection of a mound of clay spinning on the wheel. She carefully placed her hands on the clay and then watched as the smooth, wet mound spun beneath her fingers. Her back rounded and her energy moved down her arms and into her hands. She watched very intensely, in the mirror and from above, as the form began to rise to her touch. Every fiber in her muscular body was trained on what she was doing. Suddenly the clay whirled out of control. She stopped the wheel and looked at the lumps of clay oozing through her fingers. She was discouraged, but she began again.

Hours passed. Ulysses sat quietly on the window ledge watching her every move. One by one Julie placed clay forms on the table next to her. Finally, when the sun was setting and the moon was beginning to make its ascent in the sky, she stopped. The shop was bathed in the deep blue hues of dusk. Julie was covered with clay. She analyzed the pots she had finished. Most of them were lopsided, and bulky. Julie was not happy.

"I knew this wasn't a good idea."

Ulysses knew what she meant but he asked anyway. "What wasn't a good idea?"

"This." She held up one of the forms. "The shapes are all wrong. I've lost my touch." She slumped into her chair feeling very discouraged.

"Tomorrow is another day, Julie." Ulysses tried to comfort her. "It's getting late now."

Julie looked out the window. She was surprised, but glad, that the whole day had slipped away.

As Julie returned Ulysses to his house in the snow pea barrel, she noticed that the wind was coming up, and clouds were rolling in from the horizon. She took note of that. "It looks like we might be in for a pretty breezy night, you'd better get inside."

Ulysses hurried up his little ramp and then turned and looked up at her for a moment. As he disappeared into his little house, he reassured her again, "Everything takes time, Julie. Tomorrow will be a better day. You'll see."

*   *   *   *

Deep in the night Julie was awakened by a frightening clap of thunder. She sat up with a start. Lightning cracked! The sky lit up. It terrified her.

"Oh my God, Ulysses!" she thought. She looked outside just as the wind blew the little twig house out of the barrel. It hit the deck and broke apart like a hundred tiny matchsticks. Julie jumped out of bed, flung the door open and bolted out into the storm. It was pouring rain. The wind whipped her hair straight back from her face. In moments, she was soaked to the skin.

The trellis of snow peas had collapsed and the old worn vines had folded in around it. The wind swirled around her as she made her way to the barrels. She was very frightened. "Ulysses! I'm coming," she cried out. The wind was screaming through the big tree above her. She could not hear the tiny cricket's call for help.

A loud cracking and whining sound signaled the breaking loose of a huge tree branch. She looked up just in time to see it crashing toward her shop. As if she could somehow stop it from happening, she jumped to her feet and shouted "No!" But the huge branch ripped through the roof of the shop and shattered the window. Julie started toward the shop, and then remembered— Ulysses. She had to find him. She turned back to the barrels and as carefully as she could began struggling to remove debris. She couldn't see anything but the darkness around her, and the rain and wet hair streaking across her face.

As the rain pelted down on her, she ran in the house and tried to turn the lights on. The power was out. She grabbed a flashlight and returned to the barrel. As the beam of light negotiated its way through the mud and leaves, lightning continued to crack above her in the angry night sky. Then suddenly there he was, rocking and rolling on his back and struggling against the storm. As she reached in for him, another branch tore loose from the tree and came crashing down on her. It knocked her off her feet and onto her knees. Ulysses was tossed out of her hand and into the night. It was pandemonium as she reached into the wind to save him. But, he was blown away, and out of sight.

"Ulysses!" she cried out. She stumbled to her feet, and struggled against the storm toward the field surrounding the house. She called to her little friend, but the sound of the thunder drowned out her voice. Lightning flashed across the sky. All alone again, in the darkness of a stormy night, Julie stood in the field, drenched and shivering...and calling out his name.

*   *   *   *

It was a still, gray day after a storm. Ian and Annie had come by to help Julie with the mess, but they found themselves having to console her instead. She was distraught.

Annie held Julie's hand and patted it. "Julie, you have to get a hold of yourself."

Julie did not want to be comforted. "I appreciate you guys coming to help, but I have to find him."

Annie held up her fingers and gestured the size of an inch. "Julie, he is only this big. It was a hurricane out there last night."

Ian looked at Annie for direction, not knowing what to make of Julie's despair. Annie wasn't quite sure what to do either. She was more worried about her friend than she wanted to admit, but very aware of the delicacy of the situation. She didn't want to do anything, or say anything, that would upset Julie any more.

Ian tried focusing Julie's attention on the studio. "Maybe I can get started on the roof and the window. I looked the damage over, kiddo. It's not all that bad. It won't take me long to get you rolling again."

Julie stood and headed for the door. "I have to find him."

Annie followed Julie to the door and tried to stop her from opening it. "Julie, you have to let go. Maybe that's what this is all about, letting go. If you don't, you're going to lose everything."

Julie looked insistently at Annie, saying 'get out of my way' with her eyes, and then, "That *is* what this is about, Annie. You don't understand. I shouldn't have lost him."

*   *   *   *

When Julie came in from the field she was despondent. She had not been able to find him. Ian and Annie had worked diligently to repair her studio before they left. The studio was quiet. Julie collapsed onto her work stool and stared out the window. She watched as droplets of water dripped from the leaves of the tree and the rim of the roof. They reminded her of tears, but she didn't feel like crying. Her eyes wandered to the barrels, the only remnants of her shattered friendship with the cricket. She felt a heat rising in her belly.

She grabbed a hunk of clay and slammed it on her table. She pounded the clay and then slapped it and pounded it some more. Pushing, prodding, rolling, and slamming it again into the table she tried desperately to fight back the rage. But she failed. She clenched her hands into fists and then slammed them into the clay and pounded it again. She cried out "I can't do this! I can't do this any more!"

From behind her came a wee, tiny voice with a familiar snap to it. "Won't!"

Julie couldn't believe her ears. She stood bolt upright and there he was, limp-hopping through the doorway and looking up at her.

"I can't leave you alone for a minute Maxwell, I swear."

Julie started toward him. He flipped into the air and landed directly on his back. As Julie moved in for the rescue, he flipped himself right side up. He was so delighted with himself that he did a little dance-like step.

"Ulysses! How did you do that?"

"Well, if I waited around for you to take care of things no telling what might become of me," he said pointedly, facing her down with his cricket stare.

Julie went down on one knee, near the little cricket. "I've been looking everywhere for you. Calling and calling. Where have you been?"

Ulysses ignored her question and did a little lopsided hop over to her knee and looked up at her. "Well?"

She extended her hand and raised him up near her face.

Ulysses looked her right in the eye. "The storm was a challenge, Max. I would have died out there if I hadn't figured this out. I couldn't give up." He looked all around the shop. "Kind of like you can't give up."

"Ulysses, where did you come from?"

"Are we going to go through that again?" He looked out the window and then up at Julie. She looked out the window. It was nearly nightfall. The sky was clear, and ribbons of starlight were just beginning to glisten in the dark.

"There is magic all around us, Max. It just depends on what you can see."

Julie took Ulysses into the house with her that night and put him in the hanging fern. As he disappeared into it, he sighed, "I rather miss my twig house."

"Don't worry, Ulysses, I'll make you another."

In her bed that night, Julie looked through Danny's art book at the clay cricket houses. She was intrigued. She studied the little forms. They were eerily like her old work, the best of it, only in miniature. She was fascinated. "But," she thought, "they would be impossible. You can't even master what's familiar." She touched the picture with her fingertips. "Are you afraid?" she asked herself. "Too afraid to even try?"

*   *   *   *

The discipline of working in her studio was not easy to achieve. Not having worked for so long had taken its toll on her skill. The new clay she had wasn't helping either. It was uncooperative. Resistant. She was having a very hard time.

Ulysses was watching her intently. The muscles in her neck were taut. She rolled and turned the clay. Kneading it, trying to infuse it with her energy, but still she could not find her rhythm. She raised a slab of clay over her head and slammed it to the table. Ulysses sprang into the air and disappeared.

"Oh no! Ulysses, I'm sorry! Where are you?"

"I don't know where I am, Maxwell. I can't see anything."

Julie searched the floor. "You have to be able to see something."

"If I look up, I can see the roof."

Julie crawled along the floor toward the sound of his voice. "What if you look down?"

"Black."

"Black?" She tracked his voice to a stack of rocks and stones stashed in a corner behind her bisque kiln. Julie suddenly realized what it was. She moved quickly to the rocks. She looked in the spaces between them until she found Ulysses. She reached down, lifted him out and set him on the table. Her attention was then diverted beyond him. She stared at the rocks. "How could I have forgotten?" She lifted one stone from the pile and then another and another until she had uncovered the trap door. She lifted the door and began digging in the sandy soil beneath it. She dug faster and faster until she found the black plastic mound.

Ulysses watched from the table, "Well?"

"I can't believe it." She peeled back the plastic and stared at the large rectangle of clay. She ran her hands over it, remembering. She looked up at the little cricket searching for the meaning of this moment.

*   *   *   *

Julie marveled at how tiny the porcelain gourd shaped pot was as it spun on the center of the wheel. It was only a few inches tall, and just wide enough to slip the tips of her fingers into. She liked working on it. It required a whole new kind of tension in her arms and fingers. On the table around her were other miniature pots, some that had not turned out so well, and others that were perfect.

Ulysses was at the window pondering the tree. Julie looked up at it too. Many times she had felt like hugging that old tree and one of them was now. She would be hard-pressed to count the number of hours, the number of days she had kept company with that tree. How many sunrises and sunsets, storms and soft breezes they had shared. And now the wise old matron was calling—beckoning to the little cricket, challenging him to resume his life.

Magical, mystical tree, I thank you, Julie thought to herself. "You could take that tree," she said to her little friend.

No response.

She persisted, "You could. That's what those pretty little wings are for. Flying. You know, pump, pump, pump and off you go!"

"Who asked you, anyway?" he snapped back at her.

"Admit it," she persisted. "You spend a lot of time wishing you were up in that tree."

"I'm not wishing I was UP in anything."

Just then Annie knocked on the window and smiled. "Hi!" she said as she came through the door. She looked around. "Hey, who were you talking to?"

"Um...."

Then Annie noticed Ulysses sitting on the window ledge. "He's back."

Julie grinned at her friend's dismay. "He is. Isn't it great? Say hi to Annie, Ulysses."

Annie was obviously annoyed.

Julie laughed. "God Annie, do you have to take everything so seriously all the time?"

Annie shrugged her comment off and said, "Well, at least you're back to work."

Julie smiled and held one of the little pots up for Annie to see.

"Wow. It's precious. It's so little." Annie was truly amazed. " Are you going to carve it?"

Julie shook her head no. "Not yet, I'm trying these out to make a new house for Ulysses."

Annie's brow furrowed. "I thought you only had a few weeks to get ready for the show?"

Julie got up and showed Annie the book that Danny had given her.

Annie didn't want to hear anything or see anything else that had to do with crickets. She snubbed the book with a "So?"

"So, aren't they beautiful? A cricket is a good omen, Annie. Do you know there is a ton of cricket history in China?"

"This isn't China."

"No, really, just listen for a minute. They are revered. The Chinese believe that crickets can be the incarnations of great warriors and heroes."

"Julie."

"God, even Charles Dickens said that all crickets are potent spirits."

"You're not trying to tell me that someone is living inside this cricket of yours, are you?"

"Have a little imagination, Ann."

"For a bug?"

"For Pete's sake, if the Chinese hadn't been so fascinated with bugs you wouldn't have that silk shirt you're wearing." Julie raised Ulysses on her finger so Annie could get a better look at him.

Ulysses looked at Annie with one of his penetrating stares. It unnerved her and made her feel defensive.

Annie glared back at him for a moment and then realized what she was doing and snapped, "I don't care what you say, Julie, having a relationship with a cricket is pretty weird." Then she shrugged off the cricket's stare and changed the subject. "I came by because Ian and I were wondering what you are doing for Thanksgiving."

Julie winked at Ulysses, set him back on the window ledge and went back to her work. "I'm supposed to go down to Tony's mother's, but I'm really dreading it."

Annie knew she might be moving into a difficult area here, but she asked anyway, "Not ready for that much family?"

"That, and I do have a lot to do to get ready for the show."

"Why don't you just tell her that? She'll understand. Then you can spend the day with us."

Julie was tempted, but she just wasn't sure.

Annie smiled at Julie and then turned her nose up at Ulysses. "Oh all right," she sighed, "I guess you can bring *him* along."

Julie laughed. "I know you think he is a big joke Annie, but I've accepted that about you." They both giggled. Then Julie got very quiet. She thought about what she was about to say, evaluating whether she wanted to say it or not, and then she stopped her wheel and looked at Annie, "I don't think I have the courage to tell Maggie I'm not coming. She wouldn't understand about the show. She and Tony senior never considered me a real artist."

Julie's mood grew more somber with every word she spoke. "No one ever really did, except Tony."

"I didn't mean to upset you, Jule. I'm sorry I brought it up. But think about it, okay? We'd love to have you with us."

"I know, Annie, I'll be all right. I'm just going to have to get through the holidays the best I can."

*   *   *   *

When Julie filled the drying cabinet with the array of clay forms she had produced, and saw all the work lined up on the shelves, she became a little concerned. There were so many more of the miniatures than there were of the ones she needed for Zack. Maybe Annie was right. If she didn't buckle down and do some real work here she wasn't going to be ready for the show, and then what? She started her wheel up again.

Ulysses was on the windowsill, still fixated on the tree. She much preferred focusing on him, than herself. "Life is flying, excuse the pun, right by you and you're not doing anything about it," she gently reprimanded him.

He looked up at her and actually frowned. "Don't you ever give up?"

"Yesterday you told me not to give up. So which is it—give up or don't give up?"

Ulysses decided to ignore her, but she went on. "I'm only trying to tell you something for your own good. I know what I'm talking about here. Look at me. I wanted to be a successful artist right alongside Tony. But I never really tried. Then, before I knew it, it was over. Honestly, what's the point of not flying?"

"The point is I am not going to tear myself up any more than I already have just because you think I'd like to be flying. Who needs it? Life is..."

"Boring, and you are just barely tolerating it! Change isn't easy. We *know* that." She emphasized what she had just said with a 'don't we now' glance in Ulysses' direction, and then went on. "It takes a lot of hard work and even then, in the end, you might fail." Julie stopped her wheel and thought about what she had just said.

Ulysses interrupted her thoughts. "It's a long way to the ground from the top of that tree, Maxwell. What if I ripped off one of my wings on the way down?"

Julie examined the clay form she was working on and then looked down at her tools. This pot needed finish work. Hesitantly she picked up a rib tool. "So what if you did, you never use them anyway," she snapped back at him.

Ulysses went back to ignoring her.

She started trimming the lip of the little pot she was holding in her hand, but continued to prod him about his wings. "It's true, isn't it? Every night I listen, hoping you will at least use them to sing with. That maybe there will be a little chirruping around here."

"Maybe I'm not moved to sing anymore. Did that ever occur to you? And wait just a minute here. You're not so brave. What about this Thanksgiving thing?"

This time Julie didn't respond. She was concentrating on her work.

Now he persisted, "Well?"

Just then the rib slipped and made a slice in the pot. "Damn, this clay is too wet!" She reached for the small potter's torch at her side and ignited it.

The blast from the torch caught Ulysses off guard and he instinctively sprang across the room. He landed right side up, but he was too unnerved to notice. "What's the matter with you," he shouted at her, "scaring me like that!"

"I didn't mean to," she apologized. And then she noticed. She pointed at him and exclaimed, "Hey!"

"I don't have to worry about flying," he grumbled. "I'm not going to live that long!"

Julie laughed and pointed at him insistently. "Ulysses."

"Bug off!" he snapped.

Julie cracked up when he said that, which made him even madder.

"Bug off," she sputtered, "you said bug off." She pointed at him again as if to say, "would you look at yourself," but he was still in a tizzy.

"Stop pointing at me! I can't stand that pitiful, patronizing finger of yours."

Julie looked down at her finger and then at him. "You better stop your mouth and start your ears, buddy. In case you hadn't noticed...."

Ulysses was suddenly aware, "I'm right side up!"

*   *   *   *

Tilted back in her chair with her long legs extended and crossed in front of her, Julie was very carefully and precisely carving a pot. The small clay form she had cupped in the palm of her hand was extremely delicate. She punctured the form. "Damn." She set it down and picked up another. Within seconds, she had punctured it too. Within moments, another.

"Damn. I swear this borders on masochism," she said out loud. She was about to start heaving the clay forms through the open door of her studio when she heard a little clicking sound behind her and turned to see what it was.

Ulysses was using the wedging table as a makeshift speedway. He was practicing his jumping. Julie watched him covertly. At first he landed on his back every time and had to flip himself over, but then gradually he began to land right side up each time.

"Hey, you are getting pretty good at that," she praised him.

"Practice makes perfect, Maxwell."

Knowing full well what he was referring to, Julie mocked him very sarcastically, "Practice makes perfect, Maxwell."

Ulysses moved to the edge of the table, sized up the floor below, and flipped into the air. Julie gasped but couldn't look. Instead she made idle conversation. "Know what I was thinking about? My lunch with Maggie. I wonder if I'm ever going to have the courage to...."

But Ulysses had leapt successfully across the floor and landed squarely on her knee. He interrupted her with a crisp little, "Nothing ventured, nothing gained."

"My God, you've done it!"

"That's right, and I'm going to do it again." Then, looking like a tiny torpedo—a little spiraling bullet, he sprang back toward the table. "Like I said Max, practice makes perfect, practice makes perfect."

Julie looked down at her little pots and then started back to work.

*   *   *   *

At the end of the day, as Julie packed up the boxes for Zack, she nervously looked over her work. She examined the difference between the pieces she was making for the show and the little ones she had placed on the shelf. She picked up the one she had made especially for Ulysses. It looked like a jewel it was so perfect. It was very round, like a tiny teapot. She had carved a little one-legged cricket in flight on the lid and cut a special window in the front so he could get in and out on his own. There was something about these little ones, something. "Too bad Zack doesn't want miniatures," she thought to herself.

That night, she put the tiny porcelain house in the fern for Ulysses. Ulysses was very pleased.

In her bedroom, Julie settled into bed and reached up to turn out the light. Then she heard something. It was the odd little sound. Then it stopped. She listened for more. Nothing. She turned out the light and nestled into her pillow. She heard it again. She got out of bed and went to the bedroom door to listen. It was the odd little sound, but it had changed. Now it sounded like the tinkling of a small bell…hesitant at first, but then it seemed to grow more confident. Soon it was a high melodic trill, a haunting song. It was Ulysses. He was singing in his house.

*   *   *   *

Julie's meeting with Zack was not going as well as she would have liked. As he looked over the work she had brought in, a buzzer signaling him that he had a call was unrelenting. Finally, in a very perfunctory tone, he said, "I can tell you haven't hit your stride yet, Julie." Then he hurriedly tagged three pieces and said, "But, these are nice, I'll keep them."

Only three. Julie was very disappointed.

"Look, will you excuse me for a minute?" Zack said curtly, and then without waiting for an answer, "I have to take this. I'll meet you downstairs."

Julie felt sick to her stomach as she gathered up her things. Zack was chatting away on the phone like she wasn't even there. Something about some polo match. It was an awkward moment. She didn't know if she had been scolded, brushed off or discharged.

Outside, as she was loading her boxes in the trunk of her car, Ulysses popped out from under her collar. "Maybe he would like the little ones, Julie."

Julie dismissed the idea with the click of her tongue. It was too ridiculous to even consider.

Ulysses pressed on. "Well, he might. I'll bet he's never seen any-thing quite as..." he thought for a moment and then said, "as original as my house."

"So what are you now, an art aficionado?" Julie was feeling defeated. She headed back to the gallery. "Disappear, would you please," she snapped at him, and Ulysses obediently ducked out of sight.

Zack was alone in his office, and still on the phone. The con-versation, however, had taken a turn for the worse. "What the hell does Edward know about anything?" Zack laughed a snide little laugh. "He's only an artist. He either does it my way, or he takes his crap out of my gallery."

As Julie walked through the door, Zack changed his demeanor like a chameleon changing its colors. He smiled up at her and very politely hurried the caller off the phone. As he stood and walked around the desk toward her he reassuringly said, "I know this is going to be a rush for you, Julie, but you can do it. I'll tell you what, I'll come out and pick up the next batch. It will save you a trip in to the city and I'll get a chance to see where my most prized artist lives and works."

Julie was feeling very insecure. She was sinking deeper into doubt about herself and her talent. "Are you sure you want to go to all that trouble?"

"Of course I'm sure. Julie, you're not upset because I didn't want all of the things you brought today, are you?"

"Well, do you still want me in the show?"

Zack unexpectedly took Julie's chin in his hand. It was a very intimate gesture. "Don't be silly. Even at your not-so-best, you're way ahead of everyone else. Relax. You know you can do better, and you will. When I introduce you to the art world..." He stopped for a moment and gazed into her eyes as though he was very taken with her. The moment was broken by the odd little sound.

Zack was surprised by it. "What was that?"

Julie began to panic. "What was what?"

Another odd little sound.

"That. That weird little noise." Zack sort of peered around her at the back of her collar."

"My watch." Julie blurted out. "It's my watch." And then looking down at her watch she said, "And oh my, I'm late, I'm late for my lunch with Maggie." As she backed hurriedly out of his office, she sputtered, "Zack, uh, thanks. I'll... I'll call you when I'm ready...I mean when I have more pots ready." She scrambled out of the gallery.

Outside, both Julie and Ulysses were outraged, but for different reasons. Ulysses got in the first shot. "Vulture! I don't like that guy. I'm telling you, I don't like that guy at all."

"No shit, Sherlock!" she snapped at him.

"Who?"

"Never mind. What were you thinking, Ulysses? You could have blown this whole deal."

"You better watch out for him, Julie, he's not what you think."

*   *   *   *

In the restaurant, Maggie Maxwell, a stately woman with silver hair tied neatly into a chignon at the nape of her neck, was already seated at a table when Julie arrived. They hugged and then kissed on both cheeks.

Maggie started the conversation. "How are you, dear?"

"I'm fine, Maggie, and you? How is Tony senior?"

"We miss you, Julie. We haven't seen you for months. I'm glad we could meet today."

"I've been very busy. I've had my work accepted for an art show on December eighth. I don't have much time to get ready."

Maggie waved her hand at a passing waiter, "We should order, Julie, don't you think?"

Julie nodded and then said quietly, "I'll have the Chef's salad and a cup of tea."

Maggie nodded her approval and smiled at the waiter and said, "I will too." Then she focused her attention back on Julie. "Of course you will be coming for Thanksgiving. We would like you to come for a nice, long visit. We're planning a real family get together. The first since," and her voice just sort of trailed off.

Julie's back stiffened. "I hadn't thought about the holidays really. This is such an important opportunity for me."

Maggie didn't like being refused. "Julie, you haven't been back since the funeral. Not for any length of time. We lost him too, you know. You could see all your old friends, start looking for a place to live. Don't you want your old job at the university back?"

"A place to live? Maggie, I'm trying to hang on to the beach house. It was our home. It's my home now."

The waiter came back to the table, served their salads and poured their tea.

"I know you won't let us down, Julie. A few days out of your life for Tony's family can't be too much to ask."

Julie began to feel guilty. Resignation was setting in. She pushed her salad around on her plate. "You're right Maggie, I'll..." But before she could finish her sentence, she heard Ulysses pipe up.

"Nothing ventured, nothing gained," he quipped.

Julie shriveled into her chair. "Damn."

Maggie was surprised and puzzled. "Damn? Damn what?"

Julie didn't respond. She was going over the situation in her mind.

Ulysses started up again, "Like I said, Maxwell, nothing ventured..."

Julie picked up the ball, "Nothing gained."

"Nothing gained?" Maggie was confused. "Julie, are you all right?"

"Yes, yes I am. I'm sorry, Maggie. I can't come for Thanksgiving. I have too much work to do. I've wanted an opportunity like this all my life. And now I have it. I have to give it my best."

"But..."

"You know, one of the reasons Tony picked the cottage was that it had a place for my studio. He believed in me, Maggie. And now I have to believe in myself."

As she left the restaurant that day, Julie was surprised by her newfound courage. She still wasn't quite sure she had done the "polite" thing, but it certainly felt like she had done the right thing. She spoke affectionately to her shoulder, "I'm beginning to think I can't take you anywhere!"

*   *   *   *

On her way home, Julie stopped at The Potter's Wheel to pick up some supplies. She was standing at the register with Danny when Celia Fontaine swept into the shop. Celia looked and dressed more like a runway model than a potter.

Without any consideration for the fact that Danny was obviously speaking to someone, Celia rushed up to him and said, "Danny, babe, I'm in such a hurry. Do me a big fave, will you?" She handed Danny a piece of paper with a list on it, and then she recognized Julie. "Julie, Julie Maxwell. Well, we haven't seen you around for a while." The competitor in Celia began to surface. "Still playing with the kids out at State?" she asked Julie with a slightly sarcastic tone.

"Celia, how are you? No, I'm not teaching anymore."

"You haven't finally given up, have you?"

"No, not exactly."

Danny didn't like where this was headed so he entered the conversation, "Julie's getting ready for Zack's too. He loves her work."

Celia was not happy to hear that news but diminished her own reaction with a snippy, "Still doing those carved things, Julie? Danny, be sweet, won't you, and get my things together. I'm in a big hurry. Ever since I was accepted to the Craft Council I have more work than I know what to do with."

Celia pulled the sleek, leather-bound portfolio she was carrying out from under her arm and flung it open for Julie. It contained some very dramatic photographs of Celia's work. Her pots were a modern take on jasperware. Their fine, white, unglazed simplicity and their curvaceous shapes were Celia's signature. "I'm doing mostly commissioned work now, you know," Celia added as if it was important information that Julie needed to have.

Julie was intimidated, but she managed to at least pay Celia a compliment, "Your portfolio is very nice, Celia. You must be very proud." Julie began gathering up her things so she could leave.

Danny hurried around the counter to help her.

Feeling slighted, Celia chastised, "Danny, I told you I am in a big hurry."

"In a minute, Cele."

Julie tried to be cordial, "It was good seeing you again, Celia."

Celia was quick to respond. "I guess we'll be seeing more of each other now. I just took my last load over to Zack. He is so supportive." And then twisting the knife just a little, "He loved everything. I'm so relieved to be completely ready for him. It's such an important show."

Julie's spirit crumbled as she left the shop. She was nowhere near ready. Danny helped her put her supplies in the car.

"Where is your little friend today?" he asked.

Right on cue, Ulysses peeked out from under her collar.

"Don't like Cele either, eh little fella? Can't say as I blame ya."
And then to Julie, "Don't let her get to you, Jule, I'm not ready for
the show either."

Julie smiled. She enjoyed Danny's warmth.

He reached out and took her hand. "It's good seeing you more.
I've missed you, Jule."

*   *   *   *

On the way home, Julie stopped at the Post Office to pick up
the mail. When she opened her box she saw the large manila envelope with Tony's manuscript in it. She grabbed it out of the box
and hurried home. She was very excited.

At Tony's desk, Julie sat down and rifled through the phone book
looking for a number. Ulysses leap-hopped onto Tony's computer.

"I can't believe what a perfect end this is," she looked pointedly
at Ulysses, "to an otherwise very stressful day!"

"What is it?"

"Tony's manuscript. I've got to call Mr. Jessup. Now I can
make the payment and I won't lose the house." She found the
number and started to dial.

"Aren't you even going to read it?"

Julie stopped and stared at Ulysses, then at the manuscript.
Slowly, she put the phone down.

"Well?" Ulysses prodded her.

"I can't. I can't read it yet."

The afternoon became evening. The manuscript sat on the coffee table, unopened.

Night became day. The first sunlight drifted into the bedroom.
Julie was lying in bed looking at the envelope next to her, still
unopened.

She forced herself to go into her studio. She sat at her wheel, staring at the clay. She wanted to wish the clay into a form, but she couldn't.

Ulysses was sitting on the manila envelope.

Julie made a trek down to the beach and sat in the sand hugging her knees and watching the waves. Ulysses sat on her shoe. The unopened manuscript sat in the sand beside her.

Julie's face soaked up the ocean mist like a dry sponge. It was cool and soothing, like clay. She thought about her days at the beach with Tony—the great ones, and the not so great ones just before he died. Her thoughts lingered for a moment on his death. "It's been a year, one whole year," she said to Ulysses.

"You were afraid then too," the little cricket reminded her.

It was eerie how he could sense where her mind was. "I know."

"But you got through it."

"I know, and I have to get through this." She shivered. "It's getting cold. I think we'll have a fire in the fireplace tonight." She collected Ulysses, and the manuscript, and they headed for home.

That night, as the fire crackled in the woodstove, Julie sat down on the floor with her back against a chair. Ulysses settled on her knee. She tore open the envelope and took the manuscript out. She began to read.

✳   ✳   ✳   ✳

Days later, when Julie opened the front door to Zack, her eyes were red and puffy.

"Hello, Zack, come in. Thanks so much for coming all this way. I'm running a little behind schedule," she apologized.

"Hi." Zack was happy to see her, but he could tell immediately she had been crying. "Julie, what's wrong?"

"Oh nothing, I'm just having *some* of those days." She mustered a smile.

Zack put his arm around her. "I'm a good listener."

The strength of his voice and the reassurance of his arm around her made her start crying again. Zack guided her to the couch and sat down beside her. She began to tell him her tale of woe.

Much later they were sitting on the couch, half-empty coffee cups on the table in front of them. "Since I can't seem to find any-one who is willing to refinance me, and with the manuscript trashed the way it is—I either have to let them publish it and ruin Tony's name, or give up the money and lose the house. I don't know, maybe I should just let the house go." Julie had pretty much told Zack everything there was to tell.

Zack leaned back with a cat-that-ate-the-canary grin on his face. Julie mistook it for a look of discomfort. "Oh Zack, forgive me. I shouldn't be burdening you with all of this. I don't know what's wrong with me. I have no right to…"

"I'm glad you did. I think maybe we can work something out. Would you be open to being under contract to Zachariah's in repayment for a loan?"

"What? The payment is…Zack…it's so much money."

"You're worth it, Julie. And besides, it's my business to support talented artists. I want to help you. I'll call my attorney and have him draw up some papers. We'll go over everything together and then you can put all your worries behind you and just concentrate on your work."

Julie was thrilled. She couldn't believe her ears.

Before she could speak, Zack went on. "And speaking of your work, don't you have something for me to look at?"

Julie jumped up. "Oh yes. Come out to the studio. Zack, I don't know what to say. I'm so grateful. I can hardly…."

As they passed the fern, they heard the odd little sound.

"There's that sound again. What kind of watch is that?" Zack looked at her wrist. No watch. Julie tried to ignore what was happening and hurry him out the door. They heard another odd little sound. Zack looked around and noticed that it was coming from the fern. He spotted Ulysses' little house. "Julie," he said as he moved toward the tiny pot. "Did you make this?"

"Yes, it's cute isn't it?" She tried to divert him toward the door. He resisted.

"Cute? It's incredible." He reached for it and plucked it out of the fern.

"Oh Zack, don't." Julie pleaded. But it was too late. He opened it, saw Ulysses inside and automatically dumped him on the floor. Ulysses crashed to the ground, with one of his wings severely scrunched out of place.

"Oh great. Now you've done it." Julie snapped.

Zack was surprised, "It's only a bug."

"Not you, him."

Ulysses was working himself into a frenzy. "Me, what about him? What a fiend!"

Zack looked at Julie with one of those oh-boy-I've-got-a-live-one-here looks, but then promptly dismissed her in favor of examining the little treasure he had discovered.

Julie picked Ulysses up off the floor, carefully put his wing back in its place and then put him back in the fern. "It serves you right."

Zack didn't know what she was talking about. "What did you say?"

"The light," she improvised, "I said hold it up to the light."

Zack held the little pot up to the light. "God, you can see right through it. How did you ever throw something this fragile? I can't believe you made this and you keep a bug in it."

Julie opened the door for Zack and then glared over her shoulder at the fern.

Ulysses called out after her, very sarcastically, "No guts, no glory, Maxwell!"

"It's not just any bug, Zack."

In the studio, Zack stared in amazement at the collection of miniature pots on the shelf. "I can't believe you didn't show these to me sooner."

Julie was not quite sure what to do with all of this attention, "I like them, they sort of have a sentimental value, but I never thought anyone else would be interested in them."

Zack looked like someone who just had found a gold mine. "I knew you were good," he picked up one of the little pots, "but you're a genius. Julie, you have to concentrate all of your energy on these." He held the little pot up on the palm of his hand to admire it. "When you take your skill to this extreme…these, these are collector's items!"

Julie was embarrassed. She was having a hard time accepting what Zack was saying.

"I can't imagine how you carved these. Can you do all your of forms in this size?"

Julie shrugged. "I haven't tried yet."

Zack could not contain himself. "They look like blown glass. Julie, I want to show these in New York too!"

*   *   *   *

Zack was barely out of the driveway before he was on the cell phone to his attorney. "I want a contract for this new potter. Right, that's the one. And I want it so tight she'll never work for anyone else. She is going to make me a whole lot of money." Zack grinned to himself like a Cheshire cat. "No, hell no. She feels indebted to me. She thinks I discovered her. No, it'll be a long time before that happens. She is real insecure about her work." He paused and listened for a moment, and then in a frighteningly cold and calculating voice said, "Right, as in own her."

$$*\qquad*\qquad*\qquad*$$

In the morning, Julie was standing in front of the fern admiring the little house. "Zack's right. I am good."

Ulysses poked his head out and sort of snarled at the mention of Zack's name. "You better watch out for him, Julie. He's not what you think."

"Oh Ulysses."

"Don't 'oh Ulysses' me. It's that total disregard—his complete self-preoccupation."

"I need Zack, Ulysses. He is going to help me."

"No, he needs you," Ulysses said knowingly, and then ducked back into his house. "You'll see."

$$*\qquad*\qquad*\qquad*$$

As she walked toward the entrance of David's building, Julie caught sight of herself in the window glass. She noticed how much taller she looked when she stood alone. Tony's six-foot frame had always made her appear shorter. She felt excited by her reflection, proud of the way her carriage reflected her courage today. When she entered David's office this time it was in a very different spirit than the last time.

David stood to greet her, extended his hand and smiled the smile of a man who thinks he is holding all the cards. "I'm glad to see you are tending to things more promptly these days."

"David, how are you?"

"Good, good. Have a seat, Julie."

Julie declined his offer and instead stood in front of his desk, facing him.

"Would you like some coffee?" he asked.

Julie tossed the manuscript onto his desk. "No thanks, let's get right to it, David." David was surprised by the gesture. Julie went on, "I'm sure I don't have to tell you this is unacceptable, do I?"

"What do you mean, unacceptable, Julie? I told you this was business."

"I'm aware of that. It is business. My business. You have trashed Tony's work." She patted the manuscript. "This is not going to be published in his name, David. Not now, not ever."

"Julie, you don't understand."

"No, you have it wrong. I do understand. This is not his work. I don't know what you have to do to remedy this situation, but I suggest you come up with a solution as fast as you can. I'm not above getting an attorney, David."

"You can't."

"Yes, I can. And I will. If you want to bring this to a peaceful and successful resolution then I suggest you start thinking about it. Maybe a list of writers, some samples of their work, so together we can choose the right person."

David was completely taken aback as Julie turned to leave. As she opened the door, with her back to him, she dismissed him curtly. "Think about it for a day or so, David, and then get back to me."

The sound of the door slamming behind her sounded like the starting gun at the races and she felt like a brave young filly bursting out of the gates. Striding down the hallway to the elevator, she was full of herself and beaming with pride.

*   *   *   *

The heat was on. The show was foremost in Julie's mind. She moved more surely now. As she wedged the clay, every muscle in her body seemed to come alive. Her rhythm had returned. The wheel spun. Her fingers were again agile and strong. She hovered over the clay. It responded to her every touch. Julie and the clay were one.

The miniature pots were lining up. Perfect, balanced, beautiful—glistening like little jewels. Julie made room on the shelf for more. It was obvious that she was completely absorbed in her work.

Ulysses had fallen into the background. He sat in the doorway, gazing out at the field or up at the tree. The trips back and forth to the fern were becoming obligatory. Julie and he barely spoke.

Carving and sketching, sketching and carving, each piece Julie finished seemed to have a life of its own. She was inspired. She barely broke her concentration long enough to eat. The pace was frenetic. How long could it go on?

The days ran into nights, the nights ran into days. She continued to push herself at a feverish pitch. And then, gradually, the signs of wear and tear began to show on her. The phone rang constantly. She became more and more frazzled every time she had to answer it. Her hair was matted with glaze, and she was covered with clay. Exhausted, she fell into bed at night.

*   *   *   *

In the deep sleep that comes with exhaustion, Julie was dreaming. Tony was sitting beside her on the edge of the bed. He was trying to rouse her. "C'mon Max, get up...." Julie rolled over and reached across the bed.

Ulysses called to her from the fern, "C'mon Max, it's getting late."

Julie awakened with a start. She looked up at the picture of Tony on the nightstand. She remembered. She buried her head in the covers. She longed for the feeling of Tony's whisper against her ear.

"Who loves you?" he would ask her.

"You do," she would respond. "Who loves you?" she would ask back.

"You do," he would whisper, as he ever so lightly kissed her ear and they melted into an embrace.

She reached up and touched her ear.

Ulysses called out to her. "I can't sleep 'til noon and then jump start with a cup of coffee, you know,"

Julie looked at the clock. It was almost noon. "Oh no!" She jumped out of bed and raced toward the kitchen.

Ulysses was perched way out on the tip of a long fern frond, but Julie didn't pay any attention to him as she rushed past.

"Hey, have you completely forgotten about me?" he hollered after her.

She stopped, went back and got him. She took him into the kitchen and set him on the counter. As she chopped up a water chestnut for him, she cut her finger. "Dammit!" She rushed to the bathroom for a Band-Aid. She tore one open, but when she tried to put it on she was in such a state she stuck it to itself. Now she had to cut it off. She tried again. It would be more difficult to work with a bandage on her finger. She was not happy about this. Back in the kitchen, as she hurried to make her coffee, she spilled coffee grounds all over the floor. "Not today!" she screeched. "I can't handle this today!"

"Take it easy, Max. Slow down." Ulysses tried to calm her.

"I can't slow down. The show is in four days, Ulysses. I have to be ready to fire tomorrow."

In the studio, she worked at a furious pace. She was measuring and mixing a glaze when the phone rang. As she reached for the phone, she knocked the container of glaze over. The glaze spilled all over her, the table, and the floor. She groaned and slammed the phone down without finding out who it was.

"I hate glazing! Why did I ever say I would do this show?"

Ulysses was on the table looking over the disaster.

Julie grabbed a towel and tried to sop up the mess. It made a bigger mess. "Damn. Damn! Damn!!" She threw the container across the room, splattering color everywhere. She looked down at herself. An image of Tony, and the day they painted the house, appeared in her head. She shook it off. "I don't want to do this stupid show. A bunch of phony people all standing around, 'oh Miss Maxwell,'" she mimicked, 'where do you get your inspiration, your work is so exquisite.'"

"I thought you were happy about the show. It's what you've always wanted," Ulysses tried to remind her.

Julie remembered Tony holding the keys to the house just out of her reach. She heard herself telling him, "I've wanted my own studio all of my life."

Ulysses persisted, "What's the matter? Why are you so angry?"

Julie came back to the moment. "You can see I spilled my glaze. I'll be lucky if I have enough to finish. And don't call me angry just because you are bored and I don't have time to entertain you."

"But I...."

"That's right Mr. Do Nothing Cricket. You heard me. Don't try and blame me because you are afraid. This is not the accident and I'm not taking the blame." She raced out of the shop to get the hose and came bursting through the door with the water spraying full force. She scared Ulysses half to death.

"Oh boy, if I could fly. You'd never see this old do-nothing cricket again. What do you think this is, my whole life? This studio and that infernal fern?"

"It is your whole life. What else is there?" Julie had struck deeply and opened an old wound. Ulysses was very hurt. Julie remembered Tony trying to help her with her work. She heard herself talking to him, "...you're slipping away from me, Tony...." Tears filled her eyes. She came back to the moment, in anguish. "Oh Ulysses, I didn't mean that." She threw the hose down and reached out to him.

He recoiled from her. "No! I'm sick of riding on your finger. I'm sick of you letting me in, letting me out, putting me up, putting me down. And I'm sick to death of being here." He sprang into the air and disappeared.

"Ulysses."

The doorbell rang.

"I'm sorry, I didn't mean it."

The doorbell rang again, insistently. She ran to get it.

When she came back into the studio she was carrying a huge gift basket. It was filled with fruit and cheese and flowers and champagne and a large white envelope. Julie opened the card that was pinned to the wrapping. It said, "To my new resident artist."

She crumbled into her chair and cried. "It wasn't supposed to be like this. I can't do this without you."

Ulysses poked his head out from behind a pot. He moved toward her and climbed onto her wrist. She barely whispered, "Ulysses, I'm so sorry. I just miss him so much. I want him here with me."

"He is with you. Every time you remember him, Julie, he is with you again. He will always be with you no matter where you are. You have come very far on your own, Max. You can't let..." The little cricket's voice faded into an echo.

In Julie's mind Tony was telling her, "Promise me Max, you won't let anything hold you back." Julie looked at Ulysses and then closed her eyes, trying to hold on to the memory for one more moment.

"Nothing ever really ends, Julie," he reminded her.

And then she opened her eyes and finished it for him, "Something new just begins."

*   *   *   *

Firing day. Handling each piece with the utmost of care, Julie loaded the kiln. As she lifted each pot in her hand she scrutinized every aspect of it. They were all so delicate, so fragile. If the fire wasn't just right....

She bricked up the opening, and then paused for a moment. She took a deep breath, closed her eyes, and then tilted her head ever so slightly upward. She was in an almost ceremonial state. She reached down and turned the gas on. The jets ignited and roared as they filled the kiln with fire. Julie looked down at Ulysses on her shoulder.

"Flight!" he smiled up at her, and her face flushed with excitement.

*   *   *   *

When Julie finally had time to sit down and open the envelope from Zack, and read her new contract, she seemed to both understand and not understand what she was reading. She needed a second opinion.

At the Potter's Wheel, Danny handed the contract back to Julie shaking his head. "I'm sorry to say this, but I'm not surprised. It's his way of letting you know he intends to be both mentor and manager. He's offered you just enough to keep you going, but he'll be the one making all the money."

"I don't know what to do, Danny. I have to pay the bank or it's goodbye to the house."

"Zack is going to put expensive tags on your work, Julie. Have you thought about how much you would make if everything sold?"

"With the money from my folks I'd be able to make the payment, but that's not realistic."

"Why isn't it? Everyone who is anyone will be at this show, and they'll buy. I think I'd wait for the red dot review before I made any decisions." Danny reached up to her shoulder and Ulysses hopped onto his finger. "And what about you, little fella, what do you think?"

Ulysses liked this guy.

Julie was in a quandary. "Zack says there isn't any selling at the show."

But Danny is in the know. "No selling? No money changes hands, but people reserve the things they intend to buy."

Julie figures it out. "So that's the red dot review?"

"Exactly, everything that is reserved is marked with a little red sticker. By the end of the night you can usually count your chickens."

As Julie and Ulysses were leaving Danny's, she defended herself, almost to herself. "I can't risk losing the house. Even if he isn't the nicest guy, he is giving me a start."

Ulysses shook his head in dismay.

Julie was going to have to reach very deep inside to find the courage for this.

*   *   *   *

The night of the show finally arrived. Julie was a nervous wreck. Excited, frightened, and a little frantic, she readied herself for the big event. There was a knock at the door. She gathered up her coat. Ulysses ducked under her collar. "Don't you dare make a scene," she warned him.

He teasingly did not respond.

"You promised, dammit, and I know you are a man of your word."

On the drive into the city, Julie, Ian and Annie were filled with anticipation about the coming event. The excitement they were all feeling was contagious. Ulysses could not contain himself. He popped out from his hiding place and into full view on Julie's shoulder.

Annie was in the midst of reassuring Julie about Zack. "I think in the long run you will be glad you signed with him, his gallery in New York is..." Mid sentence Annie spotted Ulysses. She couldn't believe her eyes. "Julie! Ian, she has that damn cricket with her."

Julie whipped her head around. "I asked you not to make a scene."

Ian turned around just in time to see Ulysses disappear under her collar. "He does understand."

Annie stared at Julie in horror. Julie warded her off, "Don't say it, Annie. No he doesn't, Ian. He obviously does not understand English. Annie, just put it out of your head. Forget you saw him."

"Forget I saw him. You have to be kidding. It's only the biggest night of your life, and you're going to make a fool of yourself."

Julie directed her voice toward her shoulder very emphatically, "No one else is going to see him." And then to her friend, "You know Annie, if I hadn't started making those little pots...."

*   *   *   *

The whole street in front of Zachariah's was lit up for the holidays. The gallery glistened like a diamond. Julie stood in front of the huge window for a moment. Alone. Beautiful twinkling lights surrounded the twenty-foot Christmas tree inside. Ulysses came

out on her shoulder and Julie smiled down at him. When she
looked back at the window she saw Tony's reflection standing
next to her. For one brief moment, the past, the present and the
future all came together. She reached out and touched the window
and the reflection faded. When she looked at her shoulder Ulysses
had retreated to her collar.

Inside, the gallery was decorated with gold and white Christmas
garlands and ornaments. There was soft classical Christmas music
being played by a chamber quartet and a great banquet table that
was lush with hors d'oeuvres. There were dozens of waiters, all in
black-tie, anxious to begin serving the champagne.

As soon as he saw her come into the gallery, Zack approached
Julie. "Julie." He hugged her and Euro-kissed her on both cheeks.
Ian and Annie exchanged looks and then rolled their eyes.

"Zack, I'd like you to meet my friends, Ian and Annie
MacFarland. Ian, Annie, this is Zachary Thomas."

Zack barely acknowledged the introduction. "Have you seen
your display?" She hadn't. Zack led them through the gallery
toward Julie's area. All of the artists had their own section of the
gallery, and their works were shown in ways that accentuated the
essence of each piece. Whether it was lighting, color, wall space,
floor space, accessories or shelving, Zack had a keen eye for
detail. If nothing else, he was a true connoisseur of good art, and
a great showman.

Julie was almost overcome with joy as she approached her display. Strategically positioned as the centerpiece of the whole show,
it was like a miniature gallery within the gallery—small shelves,
miniature glass cases and tiny pedestals, everything specially con-
structed to fit the size of her work. Instead of being lost in the
enormity of the gallery, her pieces were highlighted, illuminated
and certain to be the focus of everyone's attention.

"I've fantasized about this for so long. I can hardly believe I'm here."

Zack possessively encircled her waist with his arm. "Believe it. You are going to become a star tonight. Did you bring the contract?"

She extricated herself from his grasp as graciously as she could and reached into her bag for the envelope containing the contract. She hesitated, and then handed it to him.

"Zack, there is something I have to tell you."

Zack snatched the contract out of Julie's hand. He attempted another kiss but Julie was not up for it. She deflected it by turning toward Annie.

Zack ignored her rebuff, neatly tucked the envelope away in his lapel pocket and smiled a triumphant smile.

Julie forced a smile and then tried again to speak, "We'll have to talk…"

But Zack was no longer interested in anything that Julie had to say. He was already making his way through the crowd, waving at another artist.

As Julie watched him walk away, a sense of relief came across her face. Then, she spotted Danny. "Annie, look, there's Danny. We should say hello before it gets too hectic."

"Zack is amazing, Julie, he is such a powerful man."

Julie just shook her head and led Annie across the gallery to meet Danny.

*   *   *   *

The gallery filled quickly with guests. Before long it was packed with hundreds of people. There was no shortage of glitz, glamour, or Rolex watches in this crowd.

In her display area, Julie was talking with a man and a woman when the woman accidentally spilled her champagne. Julie jumped back to avoid being drenched and bumped into the person behind her. Ulysses was jolted by the collision and came out from under her collar to see what was happening.

The woman who spilled her champagne shrieked, "What is that thing? Harold, get it off of her!!"

Julie's heart sank, "It's okay, he's..."

Harold tried to grab Ulysses. Ulysses scrambled to get away, lost his balance and fell to the floor.

Julie began to panic. "Oh God." She looked down, but all she could see was a terrible tangle of milling legs and feet. "Don't move!" she shouted. "Don't anyone move!" She dropped to the floor. People were closing in to see what all the commotion was about. Zack came storming through the crowd. Julie crawled around on the floor trying to find Ulysses.

Zack was very upset. "Julie, what are you doing?"

Out of the corner of his eye, Zack saw Ulysses hopping frantically about. He tried to crush him with his foot, but he missed. He reached down and grabbed Julie by the arm and tried to yank her up. "Julie. Get up. I won't have this in my gallery. You're making a spectacle of yourself."

Julie shook her arm free and reached for Ulysses. Zack tried to stomp on him again. Julie glared up at him and snarled, "Zack, stop!"

"Get a grip Julie, you are disrupting the entire evening. It's a bug for God's sake. Get off the floor."

When Julie looked back at the floor, Ulysses was gone. She scrambled around frantically, shoving people out of the way. Suddenly, a closed hand came through the tangle of legs and opened to reveal the terrified little cricket. Danny's voice swirled around Julie like a warm wind, "This little guy better learn to fly."

Julie's face lit up with the recognition of a kindred spirit. She reached out to take Ulysses from him. For a moment, as their fingertips touched, Julie and Danny hesitated.

Zack's angry voice interrupted them. "Julie, I said get up." He pulled her up by her arm. She was greeted by a lot of cold and confused stares. During all the commotion her parents had arrived, and so had her in-laws. Annie tossed her a "you've blown it now" look. Zack firmly tried to escort her away.

Again, she shook her arm free. "Let go of me," she insisted. "Just a minute here, Zack." She collected herself, and then looked squarely into his face, "You're going to have to excuse me for a moment." She left the crowd and headed for the door.

She heard the man named Harold behind her, "It was green and weird looking. Some sort of live insect."

Julie was so embarrassed and angry she wanted to run away and never come back. When she got to the car and opened her hand, Ulysses was trembling in her palm. He looked up at her with utter despair. Her heart hurt now more for him than it did for herself.

"Look," she reassured him, "we should have known better. You're safe now and after tonight things will be better, I promise. Things will be like they used to be." She set the little cricket down on the seat and tried to reassure him again, "I won't be inside much longer, Ulysses, I'm done with this place." She jiggled her hand and smiled at him, "Or should I say this place is done with us?" But she couldn't get a rise out of him.

He wasn't listening. He had withdrawn into himself. He retreated into the shadow of the armrest. For an instant he seemed different—more cricket-like than ever before. She hesitated, and then shook off the fear. "Don't worry my friend, we'll be back home before you know it."

* * * *

As Julie re-entered the gallery, she was greeted by her mother, a plain woman with a kind of Harriet Nelson innocence about her. "Julie, what was all the commotion about? What's this nonsense about some green bug you take everywhere you go?"

"Oh mom, I don't know what they're talking about. I think the woman who spilled her champagne just had too much to drink."

"Well," her mother relaxed, "there are some pretty unusual people here tonight. I'm so happy to see you, dear. Your father and I are very proud. We had no idea it would be such a gala affair."

Julie and her mother hugged, and Julie encouraged her to go in and see the rest of the gallery. "There are so many talented artists showing their work here, Mom."

Just as her mother walked away Danny came up and took Julie's hand. It felt so good that she clung to it. She started to tell him how much she appreciated what he had done, but a well-heeled young woman walked up and interrupted them by handing Julie a business card. "Miss Maxwell, my name is Stephanie Bingham. I'm an agent and I'd be very interested in talking to you about your work."

Julie smiled and took the card. "Of course, Miss Bingham. I'd be happy to give you a call."

Danny gave Julie's hand a little tug and pulled her toward the showroom floor.

"I'm not going to survive this night," she told him.

He leaned in close to her face and said softly, "I think you will. The red dot review is in."

In Julie's display area, all of her pieces had little red stickers on them. She could not believe her eyes.

As if from nowhere, Zack appeared behind her like a cobra ready to strike its prey. "A pretty stunning showing for a first timer, don't you think?"

Julie turned and faced him. "Zack, I appreciate what you have done for me, but your price is a little steeper than I want to pay."

Zack wasn't even fazed. "We have a contract."

Julie reached up and patted Zack's lapel pocket. "Well, not exactly. That's what I was trying to tell you earlier, but you were too busy to listen. I didn't sign it." She looked over at Danny, who gave her a smile of reassurance. "Your price is a too high, Zack," she continued, "so I have decided to try working on my own for a little while."

*   *   *   *

When Julie got back to the car, Ulysses was crouched in the same place she left him. She picked him up as gently as she could and tucked him into the warmth beneath her collar. It was after two in the morning when she finally closed the door of her house behind her and kicked off her shoes.

"The fern please," he said in his smallest voice.

She lifted him to the fern and knew intuitively it was time to be quiet.

*   *   *   *

Early the next morning, before she had even had her coffee, Julie rummaged around in her closet looking for something. She smiled when she found it, and then sat down on the bed and unrolled it at her feet. Tony's butterfly kite. She remembered back to that day on the beach. She remembered how spectacular the kite looked with the sun shining through it. She could see Tony running down the beach with it trailing behind him. She looked up from the floor and stared at the wall. She wondered for a moment if she would ever feel that way again. "I will always love you, Tony. Wherever you are, come fly with us today."

In the living room, a few minutes later, Julie tried to coax Ulysses out of his house. "Do you even know what a kite is?"

"Do I even care?"

"Don't be such a drag."

"A drag?!"

*   *   *   *

As she ran through the dunes toward the beach, Julie juggled the kite and the string roller and tried not to knock Ulysses from her shoulder.

He was protesting the entire time. "Hey! Watch it. I don't think this was such a good idea."

"Fear, Ulysses. It paralyzes you. Relax. Turn around and watch the kite. Maybe you'll learn something."

"Very funny, Maxwell."

Julie started jogging down the beach, releasing the kite string behind her. The kite dipped and bobbed and finally lifted off on the breeze. As it started to climb, Ulysses suddenly sprang into the air and took flight. Julie turned just in time to see him pumping his tiny wings and soaring up toward the kite.

"That's it!" Julie cheered. "You've done it." She watched as he darted about and chased the kite.

"I can fly," he shouted, "I can fly!" And he darted and dashed, and dove and soared, just like the kite.

As Julie watched, she felt an old familiar panic rising inside her. She felt weak in her knees and suddenly lightheaded. She stopped and sat down in the sand. Tightening her grasp of the kite string, she pulled it close to her heart. She watched the little cricket imitate the kite. And then, Ulysses buzzed around her and tumbled onto her shoulder.

She laughed and looked down at him. He had that look again. That look that said he was just a cricket. Julie shook the feeling off again. He sat there quietly, ever so quietly, and together they watched the kite climb higher and higher. It looked small now, and it was very far away.

Finally, Ulysses whispered the dare, "Let it go, Max, let it go."

"Should I? Should I, Ulysses?" She stared up at the kite bouncing along on the wind above her. She held tightly to the string for one more moment and then, yes! She let it drop from her hand. The kite floated away into the sky and disappeared.

Just when it was completely out of sight, Ulysses sprang into the air, circled around Julie's head, and darted off toward the house. "I can fly away home, Max."

"I'll race you," she challenged, and jumped up and chased after the little glistening blur she loved so much. And then, the panic started to rise again. What did he mean fly away home? As she ran after him, she was filled with dread. Had the time come? Was he going home? She ran faster and faster and faster. She hurried through the house, flung the sliding glass door open and called out to him. "Ulysses! I won!"

The stillness on the deck told her he wasn't there. She rushed to the railing and looked up into the tree. Nothing. She searched the sky. He was not there. She heard the telephone ringing. She started toward it. But no, he might be back any second. She couldn't leave her post. Her machine picked up. It was Stephanie Bingham. "There's another important show—a fantastic opportunity."

Julie smiled. "Look at me, Ulysses," she whispered into the air. "Look at me, I'm flying."

She sat down beside the barrels and closed her eyes. The breeze was blowing, the leaves were rustling, and in the distance she could hear the rolling thunder of waves breaking against the shore. She sat beside the barrel for a long time, settling into the symphony of sounds around her. She had come so far.

And then, she heard it. The odd little sound. She listened. It grew stronger. Yes. It was that high melodic trill that was his song. Ulysses was singing in the tree.

*   *   *   *

Author's Note

The journey to completion for any artist can be fraught with fear, frustration, and failure. Without the unfaltering love of my parents, and the endless support of my friends and mentors, my journey would have ended long ago. I am deeply grateful to them all.

My most heartfelt appreciation, first and foremost, goes to Nancy Crowell, my friend, my editor, and one of my greatest champions. Without her editorial skill and precision, her passion for this story and the craft of writing, her tireless work and endless encouragement, her unrelenting determination and incredible insight into the future of publishing, this book simply would not have happened.

I am also profoundly grateful to Michael Rodgerson, for opening my heart and lighting up my life with true love, laughter, and joy, for teaching me the meaning of commitment, and for reminding me always to keep on trying whenever I fail; to Carol da Silva, my forever friend, without whose love, wit and wisdom, wackiness and sensibility woven into the very essence of my life, there never could have been a Ulysses; to sweet Linda Denzer and Patty Brusher, who shared their lives, their courage, and their deaths with me, my experiences with each of them transformed me; to Julie Pickering Warner the first potter I ever knew, for having the courage to make her passion her work; to Scott Malcolm, for the exquisite beauty of his amazing little pots; to Deirdre Grover, my soul sister, for her indomitable spirit, and for loving me unconditionally, supporting me unquestioningly and making me laugh hysterically, at life and at myself; to Treacy Colbert, gifted writer and treasured friend for life, for her incomparable command of the language, for reading everything I write, no matter how rough it is, and sustaining me through my darkest and most fearful moments; to Jeanne Anderson, for listening endlessly, showing me how to let go, and helping me face myself and grow up; to Lana Gay, for her spiritual guidance and the gift of meditation, which has become my salvation, as a woman and as a writer; to Dr. Marcus Laux, true and compassionate physician, for loving what I do with his words and paying me to do it; to Marko Perko II, a great storyteller, and loyal friend, for being the best punctuation policeman in the world; to Christine Conrad, who so lovingly kept saying, "Leap if you want to be a writer, leap!"; to Kim and Steve Suvia, Lynn Silva, Natalie Neilson, Robyn Stone, and Glenn Benest, friends and mentors all, who knew about Ulysses when he was just an idea and enthusiastically encouraged me to give him life; to Patty Miller who affirms for me every day the amazing healing power of Grace; to Linda Potter, for her blazing heart and brilliant smarts; to Elizabeth von Rentzell for that one seemingly small editorial suggestion that ultimately made it all work; to K.C. Rine, Joyce Greenfield, and David Rodgers at iUniverse for their patience and fortitude in seeing this project through; to Sandy at Sandra Watt and Associates, for treating me like a real writer long before I was one; to Robert S. Anderson for capturing the essence of Ulysses with his stunning cover concept, to Matthew Wright for adding just the right touch, and to Matthew Bail for so beautifully bringing it all to fruition; to Jonni Good, the talented, gracious, sensitive, and original artist who created www.oneleggedcricket.com; to

Robert Wyman, Esq., for his friendship, generosity, wisdom, good humor, and unending patience, for always making me feel important, and for protecting me through all of my adventures; and finally, to Baba for helping me find the well, and to Gurumayi for giving me the courage to drink from it.

The realization of this book brings me great joy and a sense of fulfillment and accomplishment.

c. j. macgenn
oneleggedcricket.com